LANDON

Kate Allenton

Discover other titles by Kate Allenton

At

www.kateallenton.com

ISBN-10:
1-944237-15-1
ISBN-13:
978-1-944237-15-8

ACKNOWLEDGMENTS

I'd like to acknowledge my READERS….You all rock. Thank you for taking a chance on my books.

And a special shout out to Gayle Warnick, may you rest in peace. We'll miss you always.

Chapter 1

This assignment would be gravy they'd said. Keep the target secured by any means necessary. Not a problem. Those commands were words Landon Love lived by. He'd actually been smug about getting some downtime from the flying bullets and operatives who tried to get the upper hand. His superiors had left out one tiny, vital fact when they'd sold him on the assignment. The place he'd have to take her was the last place on earth he wanted to go. The one place he'd spent years avoiding. Home. Love Island to be exact. Local population, not counting tourists, three hundred and thirty-four, and every damn one of them knew his name.

Landon slowed his steps as he walked next to Dr. Alice Page. His gaze travelled up and down the white sterile corridor. Every muscle in his body was strung tight as he took in patients and visitors, assigning a potential threat level to each. His stomach was tied in knots. The uneasiness in his gut wasn't because of the job, or even the barrage of emotions rolling off the hospital visitors and staff making his breathing difficult. His nerves stemmed from something much worse—having to face the family he'd been avoiding for the last seven years.

Landon tugged at the collar of his shirt, making room to swallow around the lump in his throat. *Stay focused.*

Alice regarded him with somber curiosity, as if silently trying to figure him out. He'd become used to seeing the same look in her eyes, day in and day out, for the past two weeks. Today was no different.

"Things could always be worse. We could be hiding in some no-name city and stuck in a safe house with no windows."

She playfully nudged his shoulder, as if trying to lighten the mood. It wouldn't work. "We'll have the whole Island as our playground, and you have friends here. People you trust, not to mention your family. I'd call this a win, even if you're saddled playing bodyguard for me."

Family. Landon's stomach churned, and the throbbing in his head intensified. His brother, Reed, had probably tattled to his siblings and parents that he was back by now. Reed didn't know how to keep his mouth shut. It was inevitable, and only a matter of time before one or all showed up.

"I'm not here for a family reunion, Doc." He was here to work. Still, it wouldn't be long before they cornered him into Sunday lunches. Truth was they deserved an apology or two, or a million. Every family had that one odd person who didn't fit in. Landon was theirs, and he'd lived up to the cliché in every sense of the word. He was the black sheep, the odd man out. Whatever you wanted to call it. Landon was the Love who filled that role, and he performed it with expertise.

"Only one more appointment, and then we can leave."

"You don't have any more meetings on your schedule." He should know. Each person, each meeting, was vetted through the team assigned to keep her alive.

"It was a last-minute thing."

"All of your patients and meetings go through Reed so he can do background checks. You know the drill. There is no such thing as a last-minute anything where you're concerned."

"This one isn't a threat."

Alice reached for the door to her office, and Landon placed a restraining hand on her arm, effectively stopping her. "Thinking like that will get you killed. They're all threats until Reed, Avery, or I say otherwise. I'll go in first. You know the drill."

"I don't think that's necessary, but if you insist." Alice lifted her fingers to her forehead in a mock salute. It was better than the one finger goodbye he'd seen her give the last operative that she'd run off. Her lips twitched as she stepped back letting him open the door.

"Seriously?" Landon narrowed his eyes, angling his displeasure at the doctor who had just played him.

Alice stepped in behind him. "Mrs. Tanner, Mrs. Love."

His sister, Skylar, and their sister-in-law, Olivia, both rose with their hands on their backs, trying to get out of the plush fabric chairs that brought deep-chair sitting to a whole new level. Their pregnant bellies led the way.

"Dr. Parks, it's lovely to meet you." Skylar smiled and welcomed Alice with a handshake.

"Sky? What are you doing here?" Landon's brows furrowed as he closed the door behind him with a quiet click. His nightmare had officially begun. Not one Love, but two.

"It's good to see you too, baby brother."

"We're just here to meet the new doctor," Olivia answered, giving him a sugar-sweet smile, trying to lessen the tension in the room. It didn't work.

Skylar held out an envelope to Alice.

"What's this?" Alice asked and slid her finger beneath the envelope flap.

"Your own personal invitation to Reed and Avery's wedding," Skylar explained. "I know Avery would like you there, and well…we all know Landon has to stick by your side. Where you go, he goes, even if he doesn't want to. I just wanted to make extra sure he didn't miss this one like he has all the rest."

Landon could feel the weight of his sister's stare challenging him to deny the truth of what she said. His suspicion was confirmed. His brother, Reed, indeed, had a big mouth.

These two had an agenda, which was as evident as the twinkle in their eyes. And, God help him, the good doctor was like putty in their hands. Landon watched Alice's curiosity take hold. She was intrigued, which meant only one thing. Landon was fucked.

A wave of disappointment emanated from Alice and washed over him, clinging to his skin and soaking into every pore. His chest tightened at the familiar feeling, one he hadn't experienced in years.

Alice gave a little nod. "I wouldn't miss it for the world." She moved closer to Landon's side. "I don't know if you guys know this or not, but Landon, Avery, and Reed are the reason I'm still alive."

Skylar and Olivia exchanged a look that spoke volumes about what they *didn't* know.

"That's classified, Doc."

"They're your family, Landon. We can trust them." The disappointment flowing through the room, and suffocating him, swished away, lightening the pressure in his chest and easing his breath.

"Of course, you can trust us, and you can tell us all about our baby brother's heroics during Sunday lunch at our parents' house." Skylar smiled in that *you-are-not-getting-out-of-this* kind of way.

"Oh, I don't know..."

"Go ahead and give in, Alice. Skylar can be persistent." Olivia grinned and rubbed her belly. "Besides, if we're all going to be friends, you should at least get the chance to know us before you see us go into labor. I have a feeling we'll be sprouting horns when the pain kicks in."

A smile formed on Alice's lips, which quickly slipped when she met Landon's gaze. "Uh...sure. We'll try?" Her answer sounded like a question. Good.

"That's good enough for us." Oliva took Skylar's elbow, leading her toward the door. Just a few more steps and they'd be out of sight, and hopefully, out of mind.

Skylar grabbed the knob, turning at the last second. "If you can't make it, then maybe we'll come visit you." Skylar winked.

As quickly as Landon's hopes rose, they were dashed equally as fast. He knew better than to underestimate his big sister's determination. She was going to dig in her claws and try her best to keep Landon firmly grounded on this damn island.

The door clicked closed. "They seemed like nice people."

Looks could be deceiving. The truth was he honestly didn't know what to think of his family anymore. He'd been gone so long, and he'd changed so much. Maybe they'd changed too. The occasional conversations between Skylar and him had grown shorter over time, not because of her, but because of him. She'd always had a way of picking up right where they'd left off, as if the emotional strain between them vanished with each hello.

"I'm sure they are."

A twinge of guilt, hard and unyielding, lay buried in his chest. Not enough to get him to stay, but it sat there just the same. Alice was silently watching him again, like she normally did, trying to help everyone but herself, as if missing a few of the puzzle pieces needed to make it whole.

"I don't think our staying on the island is a good idea. They're a distraction."

"They're your family."

"That's my point. I should call in a transfer to a new location."

His jaw clenched, and his eyes narrowed as a mischievous grin appeared on her face. "Lighten up. It can't be that bad."

Chapter 2

"I think this is the perfect locale." Alice smiled and grabbed her purse from the locked cabinet. "Avery warned me there might be some tension."

"Ha," Landon blurted out. "That's putting it mildly. There won't be a welcoming committee. More like a family brawl."

Alice and Landon stepped out into the hallway and Alice locked her door, giving it another quick jiggle to make sure it was secure. "Let me ask you a question."

Landon kept his large, warm hand on the small of her back while leading her down the hallway. The words he wasn't saying told her he had fences that needed mending. He didn't want to stay and not because of a threat on her life. No, this was his skeleton instead of hers. Worry was etched in the fine lines at the corners of his eyes.

"What's your question?"

"What could you have possibly done to make your family mad at you?" They turned down another corridor that led to the garage parking.

"That's simple. I stayed away. I wasn't like the others who wanted to grow up here and never leave. I had plans, much bigger plans."

"Did you ever come back and visit?" she asked as he took her arm and led her into the concrete garage. She waved at the cameras as she passed, knowing hospital security and Avery were watching from the other end.

"No."

Landon opened the SUV door and stepped back, giving her room to slide in, but she paused in front of him. "Family is family, Landon. They're the only one you've got. Unless, of course, you're like me and were snatched as a baby and sold into another family. Then you'd have two."

"Alice, you don't know that yet."

"My face was probably plastered on a milk carton years ago." Someone knew. The same person who'd sent her the file. She stuffed those thoughts into a box and slammed the lid. Clearing her throat, she straightened and lifted her chin. “My point is, you can’t pick your family, and they can’t pick you. If you screwed up, then own it and apologize.”

“It’s not that simple.” Landon guided her into the SUV, as if tired of the conversation.

Nothing was ever simple. She’d learned that the hard way. Simple or not, she was going to help him. Alice might not be able to shoot a gun, or throw a decent punch, but she understood people. And Landon Love was going to get her help regardless of whether he wanted it or not. She reached for the door handle but paused before pulling it closed. His dark blue eyes were devoid of emotion, a mask she was getting accustomed to seeing.

“Start with I’m sorry and work out the rest.”

His eyes softened for a split second before he closed the door, officially cutting off their conversation. In the time she’d known Landon, she’d seen all kinds of different sides of his personality, especially the hard and demanding side when he was stressed and anxious. The other sides of his personality rarely appeared, but she’d seen them, too, in bits and pieces over time. A frown marred his lips and his shoulders deflated in sadness upon seeing his sister and sister-in-law. She didn’t miss much. He was like a chameleon, adapting to each situation, with each person. She was unsure if she'd met the side his own family knew him to be, but on Sunday, she'd see it first-hand.

The following two days, after they'd arrived, they did little else but settle into their temporary life. She split her time between working in her office, at the hospital, and self-defense training with Avery or Landon, depending on the day.

****

Alice held up her gloved hands as she watched Avery move around the mat with the style and grace of a cougar, looking for the perfect place to strike. The organization Landon worked for, The Falcon Group, had a standing arrangement to use the gym for their training arena, and today it was Avery who was dishing out Alice's future bruises. Her jailers, as she affectionately referred to them, insisted she know the basics of how to defend herself.

"What do you think I'm going to do?"

"Hurt me." Alice was quick to answer as she noticed Avery's telltale tic, a sign that she was about to hit. The hitch in her step gave her away, not that Alice had been the one to notice, but a little birdy had whispered it in her ear. Alice ducked, missing Avery's first strike.

"You're getting better," Avery said.

"Hardly." She nodded toward Avery's legs. "Landon warned me about the hitch in your step."

Avery grinned just as she dropped to a squat and swung her legs around, taking Alice by surprise. Alice landed on her back with a thud, momentarily losing the air in her lungs.

"You can use that move on your assailant to buy you some time to escape."

"I'll have to remember that." Alice groaned and reached for Avery's outstretched hand, letting Avery pull her to her feet.

"Are you nervous about lunch at the Loves'?"

"Oww. I think I pulled something." Alice moaned and leaned over, clutching her stomach, mimicking the response to contractions she'd seen in her pregnant patients.

"Alice, I'm sorry. Where are you hurt?" Avery stepped closer and laid a gentle hand on Alice's arm. Alice held her grin and slipped her foot behind Avery's. Dropping her shoulder, she shoved it into Avery's stomach. Avery landed on her ass. Her mouth parted in shock and surprise. "Well, well, well."

Alice pumped her arms, doing a victory dance around the mat. "It worked;

it actually worked! Landon taught me to play on your emotions." Alice held out her hand to help Avery up. "He warned me it might not work every time, but it never hurts to try."

"Yeah, did he teach you this?" Avery asked while sweeping Alice's feet from beneath her, effectively putting Alice again on her back.

"Nope."

"Don't ever let your guard down. You get the drop on your assailant and you get the hell out of Dodge."

"Noted."

Avery chuckled, getting back to her feet, this time not bothering to help Alice up. She grabbed two nearby towels and tossed one to Alice.

"You didn't answer my question about lunch," Avery reminded her.

"I'm not worried for me. I'm worried for Landon." Alice wiped her face and neck with the towel. "Is it going to be as bad as he thinks?"

Avery grabbed her gym bag and slid the strap up her arm. "It's possible. He's been gone a long time."

"Why didn't he come back?"

"You should ask him."

Alice placed a gentle hand on Avery's arm, stopping her from opening the door. "Help me understand so I can soften the blow. It's the least I can do for what you guys are doing for me."

A mix of emotions crossed Avery's face while she debated. "I shouldn't be telling you this." She let out a lengthy sigh. "You know Landon is ex-special forces. What you don't know is that all of the men in his unit were killed during a raid, leaving him the lone survivor. The death of friends, and people you care about, has a way of changing a man."

That little bit of information explained a lot. Her heart clenched, spreading an ache throughout her chest. "Survivor's guilt?"

Avery shrugged, but the look on her face told Alice that she knew more about Landon's secrets than she was saying.

"I need to get you back to Landon, or we're all going to be late for lunch."

Chapter 3

Landon reclined in the SUV's black leather seats and stared up at the familiar ornate, red front door of his parents' home. Memories of his brothers' disappointment, when he'd told them he was leaving, assaulted him. He could still remember the tears that his mom had shed. He'd avoided this day as long as possible. His time was up.

"Do you need me to hold your hand?" Alice asked in the quirky way that made him smile.

"I..."

The front door opened and his family emerged. Any chance of leaving evaporated right before his eyes. His brothers, brother-in-law, Sky, and Avery stepped off the porch and into the yard.

"How bad could it be?"

"Let's get this over with." Landon shoved his door open and stepped out, meeting Alice on the sidewalk. He let out a shaky sigh and guided her to where the others stood, waiting like a mob ready to be judge and jury.

"Alice, you know Skylar, Olivia, Reed, and Avery. These are my brothers, Declan and Flynn, and Skylar's husband, Luke."

"Hi. Thank you for having me."

His brothers didn't respond, never taking their eyes off Landon. The tension in the air was suffocating.

"Avery, do you mind taking Alice inside to meet mom?"

"Are you sure you wouldn't rather I stay here...you know...in case I need to pull them off of you and kick their asses for beating up my best friend?" Avery asked.

"Honey?" Reed crossed his arms over his chest. "Whose side are you on?"

"Baby, he was my best friend for years before I was ever *your* honey." Avery laced her arms around Reed. "It's part of my job, as his best friend, to have his back, even if it means against his brothers."

Landon's lips twitched. "I'll be fine."

"You're sure?" she asked.

Landon nodded, placed the palm of his hand on Alice's back, and leaned down to whisper in her ear. "I'll meet you inside."

Avery led Alice toward the house. She glanced over her shoulder one last time before shutting the door behind them.

Declan clamped his jaw tight and stared.

Landon raised his brow in challenge, meeting his brother's glare. Music blared from his parents' backyard where the party had started. This was both the last place, and the first place, he wanted to be. He clenched and unclenched his fists, waiting to see which brother would strike first.

"What, no welcome home hug?"

His brothers and Luke created a loose circle around him, leaving no viable exit. Was this what it had come to?

"Are you afraid I'm going to run or worried I'm not?"

Declan's brows dipped. "You've got some explaining to do, little brother."

"I'm sorry I didn't come home more. Is that what you want to hear?"

Waves of anger gushed from each of the men he called family, smacking Landon in the face as if they were unseen punches. The emotion seeped into his bones, filling the void where his heart used to be. Landon hated his ability. He'd been cursed with the worst of his parents' unusual DNA, with no way to turn off the onslaught of emotions that bombarded him from the people nearby. There was no hiding true feelings while in his presence, and no way to turn the knowing off.

"I said I was sorry."

"This time." Flynn's words stung, but they were true. "What happens when you disappear again?"

"Your actions affect more than just you," Reed jabbed, pushing the knife in a bit deeper.

"Not you too. You've seen me daily for the last few months." Landon shook his head at Reed, one of the other two people assigned to the little doctor.

This confrontation would be so much easier if they'd act on their anger, throw a few punches, wrestle, hell, Declan could even slap the handcuffs on him. He could deal with that. He'd preferred that much more over their unspoken words and hate.

"Look." Landon lifted his hands in surrender. "I have a job, and it keeps me away. Every one of you should understand that."

"You've missed weddings." Declan crossed his arms over his chest, the first sign the scolding wasn't over yet. Landon had to concentrate hard against rolling his eyes.

"Not everyone's." Landon grinned and gestured toward Reed. "I'm here for Reed's."

"You've missed birthdays, family reunions...you've missed things you'll never get back."

"I said I was sorry." Landon's brow rose. "I came back before my niece and nephew were born. That should count for something."

"Your apology—" Declan started to say.

"Is accepted," Skylar announced, brushing past her brothers; her oversized belly led the way.

Landon pulled her in for a hug and placed his hand on her belly. The joy emanating from Skylar cut through his brothers' anger like the brilliance from a lighthouse in the fog. "You're bigger than you were two days ago."

"And you haven't changed a bit." She grinned and ruffled his hair before linking their arms. "I'm starving, and we have a guest. You guys can continue your scowling and inquisition after we eat."

"This isn't over." Declan narrowed his eyes.

"I'm sure it's not." Landon bumped his shoulder in passing and led Skylar into their childhood home.

Alice was seated on the edge of the

patio chair with a large glass of tea on the table in front of her. She worried her bottom lip until she met Landon's gaze with an apprehensive smile. "No black eye?"

"Not yet, but it's still early." He chuckled.

"Did you apologize?" Alice whispered, lifting the glass to her lips.

"I tried."

"Good." She smiled around her sip. Her eyes sparkled with delight, and an unfamiliar, yet sweet, feeling of pride rushed from Alice, warming his skin and thawing the ice that encased him.

"Alice," Skylar announced as she approached. "Flynn's wife, Mia, just arrived, and I'd love to introduce you."

"Sure."

Reed patted Alice's arm in passing as he joined Landon and Avery at the table. He sat, pulled his chair up, and rested his arms on the table. His anxiety rolled off him in waves, making Landon's teeth ache.

"You found something?" Landon asked with a quiet voice.

"I'm monitoring some internet chatter."

"What chatter? Do I need to move her?"

"You wish." Reed shot him a lopsided grin.

Hey, a guy could dream. Things had a

way of coming full circle and biting him in the ass. The confrontation in the front yard was just the start.

"You aren't leaving before the wedding, even if I have to call in two teams to protect Alice and the people at the ceremony," Avery announced.

Reed leaned in and gave Avery such a heated kiss that it could have melted the polar ice caps. She was in love and so was Landon's brother. Unfamiliar warmth spread through Landon's chest. Envy swirled around him. Not that he wanted Avery, but the thought of a future with someone he cared about sounded nice, even if it was just a fantasy that he'd never experience. "Get a room."

Avery broke the kiss and snuck one more in before they pulled apart. "Tell Landon what you heard. He needs to know."

"Alice's DNA reports were compared to her sister's, and there is no chance that she belongs with the family that raised her."

"Shit." Landon dropped his gaze and clenched his hands. Just as Alice had thought. No matter how much she teased and pretended the answers weren't going to bother her, he knew better. He knew women.

"I see time hasn't taught you better manners." His mother's sweet voice was music to his ears.

"Momma." Landon rose and pulled his mother in for a hug. He kissed the top of her head.

"I'm glad you're home, baby," she said as a tear welled up in her eye and broke free, slipping down her face and reminding him of the time he'd left.

"And you better stay that way," his father said in the deep baritone voice that was reserved and used only during times Landon or his brothers were in trouble.

Landon released his mom and hugged his dad with a pat on the back. "I'll make a better effort."

"See that you do." He glanced around the table. "Lunch is almost ready so finish up your shop talk. We won't be having any of that at the table."

"Yes, sir," Reed answered.

They waited for their parents to retreat out of earshot. "Anything else to report?"

"There are two families that paid for the stolen babies still unaccounted for. One skipped town without a trace before a retrieval team got there, and the company is still trying to trace the other buyer."

Landon gave a slow nod as he processed the new threat. "Are you searching for them?"

"We have facial recognition running on everyone who enters the island. Even if they have fake IDs, we'll still find them,"

Avery announced as she glanced toward the open French doors. “Have you told Alice about your family’s special DNA?”

He shook his head. “There’s currently no need.”

“And how are you holding up with all the emotions at the hospital?”

“I’m dealing.” He stood as he saw his father gesture them inside.

Lunch went off as expected. Declan grilled Alice with questions and gauged each answer for the truth. Olivia and Skylar talked baby crap, and Mia and Alice became instant friends, discussing experiments and medical mumbo jumbo. Landon sat quietly, listening to the conversations around him like an outsider looking in. The tension in the room eased as the hours passed, almost disintegrating by the time they had to leave.

Chapter 4

Alice slid into the passenger seat and glanced up at the Loves' house while waiting for Landon to get in on the other side. Declan, holding a beer, stood on the porch, leaning against the rail.

"Well, that wasn't so bad."

Landon shoved the key into the ignition and started it. "It could have been worse."

"Yeah, your brother, Declan, looks like he still wants to clobber you. Does he always look like that?"

Landon chuckled. "He's the sheriff. He's paid to look like that and has been perfecting it since we were kids."

They rode in easy silence back to the house the company had deemed their safe house. It was the only two-story brick building that included a safe room, and it sat nestled in a clearing on the other side of the island. A picturesque lake graced the landscape in the back yard, with a dense forest surrounding the lake and the house. Landon and Avery had assured Alice that no one was coming or going without an alarm being tripped. She was supposed to feel safe in this new place, and yet the big house felt overwhelming.

Landon pulled down the driveway.

"Who is that?" She gestured to the man sitting on their steps holding a manila file in his grasp.

"Miles Phillips," Landon grumbled in a tone not the least bit happy. "Another operative who wanted your detail."

"That can't be good, right?" Alice asked, trying to mask the unease in her voice. Miles was a good-looking man. He was dressed in fatigues and a black T-shirt that stretched across his chest. Tattoos peeked from beneath his sleeves. He had that same commando vibe that oozed from Landon. He ran his hand through his military-cut brown hair. His dark eyes were glued to their vehicle.

Miles rose to his feet as Landon and Alice got out of the SUV and headed in his direction.

"What are you doing here?" Landon asked, bypassing the operative and slipping his key into the lock. He punched in the alarm code on the house before repeating it in his cell phone.

"Hello, I'm Alice." Alice extended her hand.

"I'm Miles." He shook her hand. His eyes twinkled as he held her hand a bit too long. She slipped her fingers away. An uneasiness wrapped around her body. Maybe it was just because he was yet another reminder that Alice wasn't on the island for a vacation.

****

"Let's move this inside. She's an open target out here." Landon gestured toward the open door and waited for her to pass before stepping in front of Miles and blocking his entrance. A whiff of arrogance hovered around Miles, as if it was a permanent part of his aura. "What are you doing here?"

"I'll start the coffee, and you two can talk about whatever was so important that he had to drive all this way."

"It appears I'm having coffee." An easy smile played at the corners of his mouth.

Landon reminded himself that Miles had to have come for a reason. He'd get the intel and then tell him to get the hell out. He stepped out of the way, and they both followed her into the kitchen, where she started a pot of coffee.

"I'm sure you know two of the families are unaccounted for. We found one...sort of."

"You got a hit on the family that ran?"

Miles took a seat at the kitchen bar and slid a manila envelope to Landon. "No, we still haven't found that family. This is on the other family."

Landon opened the file to a crime scene photo. An older couple lay dead, face down on the floor, in a puddle of blood. Their hands were still bound behind their backs and secured with duct tape. He flipped to another picture of a burning car and then started reading the reports. His eyes shot up to Miles.

"You've got to be kidding me."

"Afraid not." Miles winked at Alice as she handed him the coffee mug. "That is Andrew and Claudia Perriman. They purchased one of the abducted children. It seems Junior didn't take the news of his abduction too well and took out his anger on the couple that raised him."

"You sure he did this?"

Miles pulled out the paper in the back of the file and set it on top. "Andrew Perriman, Jr. has a history of violence that the family covered up as well."

"Not too well if you found it," Alice said as she placed a mug of coffee in front of Landon and went back to fixing herself a cup.

"Well, honey, that's what we do. We find what others don't want us to find."

Alice lifted her brow. "Junior appears to be the obvious choice, but you do realize there is someone else who is just as angry at those two people as Junior probably is."

"Who?" Miles asked.

"The parents he was taken from. The question you should be asking is which one would kill in cold blood."

"Junior has a history."

"I'm sure you're right." She shrugged. "But what if Junior's psychology is linked to DNA and his real parents are just as awful?"

"And what if his tendencies are linked to his upbringing?" Miles countered and then smiled over the top of his mug.

"We can sit here and guess all day at who did this. What does the evidence tell us?" Landon asked, going straight to the root of the problem.

"The deaths happened at night. They're still analyzing the scene, but one of the neighbors police questioned saw a male, dressed in black, running from the scene."

"Junior," Miles said as if he already

had the kid convicted.

"Or Junior's biological dad," Alice mumbled and walked out of the kitchen.

Miles rolled his eyes, making Landon's lips twitch into a grin.

"She's a handful."

"You only wish she was in your hands."

"No denying that." He wiggled his brows.

"You're the last thing she needs. She's been through a lot."

"Like you're any better, Love. I'll keep you posted on the hunt for Junior."

"Thanks." Landon set down his coffee cup and walked Miles to the door. "Email Junior's picture to Avery so they can add it to their facial recognition search."

"Will do."

Landon followed Miles off the porch and walked him to his car. Miles opened the door and glanced back at the second story. "Let me know if you need help with her."

Landon glanced over his shoulder and found Alice watching them. "I've got her covered."

"I'll bet you do." Miles winked and slipped into the car without another word.

Landon watched the taillights disappear down the drive before he moved back inside, locked up, and reset the alarm.

He grabbed a beer from the fridge and settled in the office with the file in front of him. The danger for Alice was multiplying by the minute.

"You're worried about this one?" Alice leaned against the doorframe, a cup nestled in her hands as she masked the inner turmoil that swirled around her with a deceptive calm.

"Whoever did this might be carrying a vendetta against you for ruining their life or outing their involvement in the kidnappings, and we both know they're capable of killing." He held her gaze, sending out his own protective wave of emotion and letting it wrap around her. "You're safe here."

Alice had changed into shorts and a T-shirt. Her hair was pulled up in a ponytail and out of her clouded green eyes. On days when she was happy and excited, her eyes sparkled like beautiful emeralds catching the light in a room. On days when she was determined and scared, they clouded and swirled with gray specks. Her eyes were the window to her soul. Her deep greens acted like the punctuation at the end of a sentence, confirming the emotions he could feel from her.

Alice was a strong, beautiful woman. At another time, and in another place, he might have acted on his attraction to her.

That time and that place wasn't today or on the island.

She lifted her chin and stepped through the doorway. The small gesture didn't hide what he already knew from the energy in the room. She was apprehensive. This threat, unlike most of the others, was actually affecting her. Was it because she'd seen it first-hand in the photos?

"No one but the agency knows who you really are and where you're hiding."

"I know." She sat down in the chair, perching on the edge. "I'm just having a hard time with all of this. I've ruined lives by coming forward."

"You've brought peace to the families who didn't have closure. Who didn't know one way or the other if their babies were still alive or what had happened to them. That's a good thing. You were put in an impossible situation and did the right thing."

"I get that, but *who* put me in that situation? Who's pulling my strings?"

"We don't know yet," Landon answered honestly. He could feel the disappointment wafting from her. He could feel the emotional vibration in the air battling with the safe vibe he was pushing back at her.

Landon stood and rounded the desk to sit in the chair next to her. He took her small hands in his and ran the pad of his thumb over her palms. "Alice, we will get answers. It's just going to take some time."

Alice lowered her gaze to their clasped hands. Her apprehension was replaced with something worse—sadness. She lifted her gaze to meet his. "I didn't look like either of my parents, and I don't look like my sister. I know what my DNA results are going to say."

Damn, how could he have forgotten to tell her? "I'm sorry, but you were right. Avery and Reed told me the results before we ate. They compared your DNA to your sister. It's not a match."

She gave a knowing nod. Her hands momentarily trembled, and her eyes turned glassy.

"Who am I, Landon?"

Landon dropped her hand and cupped her cheek. Her skin was soft to the touch as he wiped away a tear that slid free. All he wanted was to find her answers and remove some the anguish she was trying her best to hide. "We both know who you are, even if we don't know your parents' names. You're a good person who helps anyone in need. You're caring and compassionate and have the biggest heart of anyone I've ever met. You're smart and beautiful and a damn good doctor. No one can take those things away from you."

"You think I'm beautiful?" she asked, her voice a whisper.

His lips softened into a smile. The fact

she even had to ask made her ten times more attractive in his eyes. "Any man with a half a brain would agree. Alice, I promise you; we'll find your answers."

She searched his gaze. The sadness surrounding her softened.

"Don't make promises you can't keep." She pressed her hand over his and gave it a gentle squeeze before removing it from her face. Alice stood and he rose with her. Their bodies a breath apart, the energy charged. He crossed the professional line and gathered her into his arms holding her against his chest, offering her what strength and comfort he had to give.

Her body eased into his hold as she wrapped her arms around his waist and buried her head into his throat. Seconds ticked by without words, and neither of them pulled away. His heart raced, the beat matching hers. How could anyone hurt this woman? He briefly closed his eyes, not wanting to let her go, yet he did the honorable thing and dropped his hold. Neither of them needed the complication.

"Alice." She lifted her gaze to meet his. The gray in her eyes lightened. "I promise I'll never give up trying to get your answers."

Her eyes had glazed with unshed tears before she cupped his cheek. "You're a good man, Landon Love, and I believe you."

The air between them sizzled as he lowered his gaze to her lips. The battle with his urge to kiss her weighed heavy against his chest. He had a professional duty to keep her safe, and a kiss would complicate things. A kiss would be unprofessional. A kiss...

His thoughts drifted away as Alice rose on her tiptoes and pressed her lips to his, taking the fight out of his hands. The kiss was wrong on so many levels, yet he couldn't pull himself away. He pulled her body flush with his and deepened the kiss, taking from her what she readily offered. Just this once, he'd throw caution and reasoning into the wind and just let himself feel something other than the swirling emotions. Heat flowed through his veins, awakening parts of him he'd thought long dead. She moaned as his tongue explored the recesses of her mouth. He moved his mouth over hers, devouring her softness and leaving a burning fire running through his veins. Her soft, subtle body melted in his arms. He splayed his hand against her back, holding her, nowhere near ready to let her go. The kiss was probably some emotional or psychological reaction. She'd come to her senses, even if he couldn't.

Alice broke the kiss and stepped away. Her mouth was parted, and her cheeks were flushed. Pleasure and need radiated from her. “I’m sorry. I shouldn’t have done that.”

Her gaze searched his. Was she looking for acceptance, appreciation? Whatever the hell she wanted or needed, he’d give it to her. Landon licked his lips, savoring her taste. “I’m not sorry. I should apologize and say it was unprofessional of me to kiss you back, but I’m not sorry.”

Her eyes softened, and she gave him a small smile, as if still in shock.

“I like you, Alice, but under the circumstances, no matter how badly I want to taste you again…”

“You do?”

His lips twitched. “I do, but I won’t. Not while I’m protecting you. It’s a distraction neither of us can afford.”

Regret drifted from her body as her shoulders sagged. “I’m a distraction?”

Landon stepped closer and gently touched the freckle on her neck. “This freckle is a distraction. I’ve wanted to kiss it since I met you.” He lifted her arm and ran the pad of his thumb over the birthmark on her inner arm. “And your birthmark. That’s a distraction. I’ve daydreamed about searching your body for other distractions.” He pressed a tender kiss over the mark on her inner arm. “You’re a walking distraction, and it’s hard keeping my head in the game when my thoughts drift to how it would sound to hear you moan my name."

Being with her twenty-four-seven for two weeks had done a number on his head, not to mention kept his body hard as a rock. Seeing her in the workout bra the first time, it had taken everything he had to hold back from lifting it over her head and tasting what he knew was hiding beneath. Her fire called to him, even if she didn't realize the emotions she'd sent out. He'd felt her lust and knew one touch had the ability to crush them both.

Alice visibly swallowed.

"Your sweet taste is branded on my lips." Landon ran his thumb over her birthmark once more before letting go. He eased back behind the desk, putting more room between them. "So for now, I won't act. But when this is over..." He sat back down in his chair. "I'm going to kiss you again."

"Is that a promise?" she asked. Her voice came out in a whisper.

"Another one I intend to keep."

Chapter 5

Landon's eyes shot open as the alarm wailed throughout the house. He grabbed the gun beneath his pillow, slipped out of bed, and peered out into the hallway. He aimed the gun up the hallway as he stepped out and moved across the hall to Alice's room. He opened the door to find Alice shoving her shoes on her feet. His relief was short-lived.

Landon held out his hand and she took it. He moved her to the closet and shoved the clothes aside, pressing numbers into a keypad on the wall. His only goal was to get her someplace safe.

The concrete door to the safe room slid open and he moved her inside. "We've practiced this drill. If I'm not back in twenty minutes, use the phone in here to call for help and stay put."

"Landon..." Her voice trembled as she rested her hand on the phone.

"Stay here." He pressed the numbers again, knowing the code was on the wall inside the safe room, if she needed to get back out.

She gave a hesitant nod before stepping back and letting the door close. Landon slipped from the room. His heart raced with each step he took down the hall. He completed a thorough sweep of the upstairs, checking each room, closet, and corner before he descended to the lower half of the house.

He kept his finger on the trigger and his back to the wall as he eased down the stairs and continued searching the house for the point of the intrusion. He got to the French doors in the kitchen and paused. Glass was scattered on the tile. A tree limb hung half in and half out of the opening.

Landon moved to the alarm pad by the door and turned the alarm off before slipping out of the front door. He jogged into the tree line ignoring the limbs that scratched his feet. He eased into a better position and watched the house for any movement. Anything to indicate that the limb was anything other than a freak of nature. The only sound he heard was the beating of his heart. The only movement was the breeze on the waves in the lake.

He kept a vigilant look as he headed back into the house. He picked up the phone and hit the intercom button. “Surf’s up.”

Their code word for the coast is clear. Anything other than that one phrase and she was to stay tucked away.

He hurried back up the stairs and met Alice in the hallway as he walked into his room. “What was it?”

“A limb busted through the French doors in the kitchen.”

“The wind from the coming storm?”

He shrugged, grabbed his jeans, and slid them over his boxers. Her gaze lingered, and her cheeks heated. The look was cute. She was cute. When her gaze reached his face, he couldn’t hide the silly grin on his lips. He winked before he spoke.

“The wind must have picked up while we were sleeping. The storm isn’t supposed to hit for another few days.” Landon grabbed his boots and shoved his feet inside. He slipped his phone off the dresser and dialed Avery’s number on his way back downstairs. If he didn’t know better, she was already on the way. She answered on the first ring.

"I'm in-route."

"False alarm. Tree busted the window and broke the pane."

"I'm in the driveway."

Landon glanced over his shoulder. "Avery's here. Will you let her in?"

Alice nodded and hurried out as Landon looked for a broom and dustpan to start cleaning up.

He picked up the bigger pieces and had started tossing them in the trash as Avery walked into the room. Her wrinkled clothes and tangled hair were a testament to her state before the alarm kicked on.

"I'll clean up outside," Avery said in passing and headed right back out the door.

"I'll start some coffee," Alice announced, moving through the kitchen, careful to avoid the area next to the door where Landon had swept up the small pieces. Avery opened the door and leaned inside. "Uh…Landon. Can I see you out here?"

"Sure."

Landon stepped outside to find Avery in the yard, slowly turning as she scanned the tree line, her phone pressed to her ear as she spoke.

"Yeah, check all of the monitors and call me back."

"What's up?" Landon asked as she disconnected the call.

"The limb wasn't an accident."

Landon glanced over his shoulder back at the house to find Alice standing at the kitchen sink window watching them. "What makes you say that?"

"The limb didn't break from the tree," she said, glancing up at him. "There was a straight cut."

Landon's gaze shot up to the tree line. "Anything on the monitors?"

"Reed's looking into it as we speak."

Landon gestured back to the house with his head. "Keep Alice inside while I go check things out."

She nodded and hurried back inside as Landon took the gun out of his waistband and started at a jog into the surrounding forest.

He moved silently through the trees, his gaze darting around him. Alert and on edge, he inhaled nothing but the scent of trees, no emotions but his own as he worked his way around the perimeter. He stepped onto a fallen log and paused. On the other side of the log was a single footprint. Landon pulled out his phone and dialed Avery.

"I've got a footprint to the east."

"I'll tell Reed to concentrate on those feeds."

"Stay alert," he whispered into the

phone before hitting the End button and shoving the phone back in his pocket.

Landon stepped over the log, careful not to disrupt the footprint, and stood silently listening for anything other than chirping birds and forest animals. He was met with silence. He used the light of the moon piercing through the trees to search for clues. Anything to tell them which way the intruder might have gone. Nothing.

Landon spent another forty-five minutes in the forest, searching the perimeter and the surrounding area before he headed back toward the house. He jogged up the back stairs to the patio, where Avery stood at the door with a gun in her hand.

"Did Reed find anything on the feeds?"

"They were looped. Whoever was out here knows electronics and knows how to stay out of the picture while doing it."

"Pack your bags, Alice. We're leaving."

"What?" She rose from her seat. "No, I'm not leaving. That wasn't the deal."

"I'm just going to call Reed." Avery gestured toward the living room.

"Alice." Landon took a deep breath. He didn't want to yell. It wasn't her fault that their location was blown. His body vibrated with adrenaline. "They found us. We need to move. I know you don't want to, but your life comes before your happiness."

"Says who?"

"Says me," he answered; his voice was deadly and deep. "My job is to keep you alive."

Alice held out her hands to her sides. "You're doing your job. I'm alive. I'm safe. No one got to me." She took a step in his direction. "I have a job too, Landon. People are counting on me to deliver their babies. I can't just walk away from that. Hell, I have three patients who are going to pop any minute and a possible C-section that we're monitoring."

"Alice, you aren't the only doctor on the island. Someone else can do those."

"I'm not running, Landon." Her eyes pleaded, and her determination simmered in the air like a volcano on the verge of erupting.

"It's hard to do your job if you're dead," he countered.

"I won't stop living just because you think I should. I trust you to keep me alive, and on the island, we have the home court advantage." Alice spun around and left Landon standing in the middle of the kitchen.

Damn it. Landon shook his head and turned to stare out the kitchen window. Other men had trusted him to do the same thing, and he'd failed. If he lost her...

"For what it's worth, I'd trust you too,"

Avery said from the doorway.

"You know what happened in my past." He turned and leaned his hip against the counter. "She doesn't."

Landon watched the emotions cross her face. He didn't need to feel them to know that she was hesitating.

"What aren't you telling me, Avery?"

"I kind of told her when I was explaining about what was going on with your family."

"You what!"

Alice came rushing into the room. She was dressed in scrubs and had her stethoscope around her neck. "We gotta go. The Jensen baby has decided to make an early appearance."

Avery shoved Landon to the living room. "Take her. I'll stay until the window is fixed, and when the sun comes up, I'll check the area one more time in the daylight."

As he took the stairs, he could feel his throat closing. Her refusal to leave only fueled his fears, and Landon wasn't a man who feared much. He took the stairs two at a time up to his room, returning moments later wearing a different shirt and holding his keys in his hand. A gun was strapped to his leg and another to his back.

Chapter 6

Landon pulled into the doctors' parking lot and killed the ignition. "I don't like this."

"Everything can't always be nice and tidy."

Alice opened the SUV door and hopped out. Landon was quick on her heels. His eyes darted around the dimly lit parking garage as he placed his hand on the small of her back, quickening their pace.

Alice stabbed the elevator button and then stepped to the side just as Landon had taught her. Out of sight was out of the crosshairs.

"I'm sorry you're mad." Remorse flowed

freely from her to him. "And I'm sorry about your old unit. It wasn't your fault."

"You don't know that." The doors to the elevator slid open and they stepped inside. His body and mind were tight with tension. He ran his hand through his hair and squeezed his neck. "I don't want you to be another casualty."

Alice took his hand and gave it a gentle squeeze. "You can't save everyone, Landon. Avery, Reed, and you are the only people I trust to get me through this. If you try to get me to leave, I'll run. You know I will."

He nodded, pushing away the memories of his fallen friends. She wouldn't succumb to the same fate. The elevator dinged and she pulled her fingers free and waited for him to step out, following the protocol he'd demanded and taught her in the prior weeks. He checked the hall and ushered her out, the two of them walking side by side toward the delivery area.

Alice swiped her card key, and they both walked into the restricted area. He breathed a sigh of relief that she, at least, had that little bit of security around her. Things could be worse. They could always be worse.

Alice headed directly for the busy nurses' station and grabbed the file the nurse handed her. "What room is

Jenson?"

"Delivery room 3. She's prepped and dilated seven centimeters."

Alice nodded and flipped the file open, walking on autopilot toward the room, her gaze locked on the chart, not even bothering to notice her surroundings. She paused with her hand on the door. "You'll be here when I'm done?"

He nodded, and she gave him a small smile. Stretching up on her toes, she planted a quick kiss to his lips. "I'll see you in a bit."

****

Landon paced outside the room much like an expectant father. He'd called Avery a few times and checked in with the teams working to locate the psychotic son, and to see if there were any additional viable threats. Reed had called to tell him that he'd finished reviewing the facial recognition, and no flags had gone off for anyone coming onto the island. Everyone associated with the baby snatchers was either accounted for or on the run. Whoever had been responsible was a mystery they'd need to solve. His gut coiled at the thought. The adrenaline slowly dissipating from his body made his eyes tired.

Two hours later, Avery showed up to

relieve him so he could run back to the safe house to get a shower and freshen up. He'd been gone thirty minutes when Avery called to tell him that Alice had finished and they were safe in her office. Landon let out his first relieved breath. He called in an order at the local diner and picked it up on his way back hoping with some food, and a little heart to heart, maybe he'd be able to get her to change her mind.

He juggled the coffee and bags while knocking on the office door. Avery opened it and stepped back. Alice was behind her desk. Dark bags hung beneath her red, irritated eyes. She was tired. He registered it with fresh eyes. His need to protect Alice went deeper than keeping her alive. Soon she'd break down. Her emotions were already on the verge of doing so.

"I thought we could all use something to eat."

"You're a lifesaver." Alice smiled up at him as Avery took the coffee container from his hands and passed out the cups.

"I'll take my coffee to go. I have a sexy fiancé at home who needs my help." Avery winked and headed to the door.

"I didn't know what you'd like, so I got a little bit of everything. Pancakes, eggs, cinnamon rolls, hash browns, take your pick." He heard Avery chuckle as the door clicked closed.

"I'm starving." Alice stood, helped him

open the cartons, and dished herself out some food.

"So what did she have, a boy or a girl?"

"Girl." Alice poured syrup on her pancakes. "Nine pounds eleven ounces."

The thought warmed Landon. "Did you finish your reports?"

"I did. We can leave when we're done eating. Assuming none of my other patients go into labor before we get to the car."

They ate in easy banter while Landon continued working different scenarios in his mind on how he might be able to convince her that they needed to move. Home turf or not, they were sitting ducks on the small island without many ways to escape. Landon fished his phone out of his pocket and fired off a text to Avery about putting in place some optional escape routes. With this house, and this location, it was just a matter of time before they would be leaving it all behind.

Chapter 7

Edward Best leaned against the hospital wall holding the flowers. From the corner of his eye, he watched and waited as the doc and her bodyguard approached. His heart hammered against his ribs. She was so close, and yet, still untouchable.

"I need to call Emily tonight," Alice announced as she passed by Edward. "She needs to know the DNA results."

"You know Emily loves you. She's your sister, and no report will change that. Family doesn't always have to share DNA."

"I know, but it still sucks what our parents…" Her words trailed off as they made their way farther down the corridor toward the elevator.

Emily Page, the sister the doctor had grown up with, even if not blood-related, was another reminder of the dirty deeds plaguing him. What he'd found out was that the two were as different as night and day, yet they were close, a bond he'd hoped might sever. Emily had gone to extreme lengths to find Alice, and save her life, when she turned up missing after he'd sent her the baby snatching details. A twinge of anger ripped through Edward's chest, settling in the pit of his stomach. Alice Page had a lot to learn about herself, about her family, and about him. Edward's lips twisted at the corner as he turned and headed toward the exit sign hanging above the stairwell. He pulled a single bloom from the vase, dumped the remaining flowers into the nearest trash can, and began whistling as he left. Time was of the essence. Like a game of chess, each choreographed move was taking him closer to his goal. Soon she'd know everything, and only then would the real fireworks begin.

****

Alice stepped onto the elevator and turned while Landon pressed the button. Her gaze remained fixed on the man with the bouquet of exquisite lavender roses. She met the man's gaze and held it. He was familiar. She'd seen him before. She was sure of it. She tilted her head as the doors slid closed, cutting off her view. When had she turned so paranoid? She disregarded the thought as exhaustion seeped into her bones and the food in her belly settled. He was probably just a new father, which would explain where she'd seen him. Her lack of sleep, from the alarm to the unexpected delivery, was playing with her mind.

She followed behind Landon, letting him check the SUV before he opened the passenger door for her to slide inside. Within minutes, they were on their way to the safe house, using the longer of the two varied routes as to not follow the same path back to the house. The numerous ways back to the safe house were a precaution that under normal circumstances, she would appreciate, but not today when her eyes were heavy and every bone in her body was tired.

"I'm tired, Landon. Can't we take the other way?" she asked, and her head lolled toward him. Landon's gaze darted from the road to the rearview mirror and back. This wasn't the first time she'd watched as he noticed their surroundings, though this time was different. His jaw was set in a hard line. His eyes narrowed, and he turned down the road that led tourists toward the scenic route, leaving their scheduled route behind.

"We've got company."

Alice had turned to look out the back window before Landon caught her arm and shook his head. He used the Bluetooth attached in the car system and called Avery. She answered on the first ring. Her voice filled the SUV.

"What's up?"

"We've got a potential tail."

"Where are you?"

"On Sunset, heading toward the pier."

"Reed, I need the feed from the street cams on Sunset." Avery's voice was muffled.

"He's pulling up the cams at the pier. Drive slowly or park so we can get a clean shot."

Landon pulled into the pier parking lot and then pulled into an empty parking spot that granted them a fast escape. Adrenaline shot through Alice; she was now wide-awake and had sat up straighter in her seat. Her gaze darted back and forth as she tried to figure out which vehicle Landon was talking about.

"Did he follow? We're not seeing him in the feed."

Landon's gaze shot around them and settled on the dark sports car that slowly rolled by on Sunset. "False alarm. He didn't turn in."

Alice turned her direction toward the slow-moving car. The man from the hospital corridor was behind the wheel. Maybe she wasn't as paranoid as she thought. "That's the guy from the hospital."

"You've seen him?" he asked.

"Where in the hospital?" Avery asked over the speaker.

"I noticed him when we were leaving. He was in the hallway when we got on the elevator. He was holding purple roses."

Before Landon could begin barking orders, Avery answered. "I'm on it. I'll call you back when I have an ID."

The phone went dead.

****

Fifteen minutes later, Landon turned off the main road onto the dirt road that led to the house. A ringing filled the car, alerting them that Avery had an answer to the question that had all of them on edge.

"Edward Best," she announced without preamble after the first hello. She continued. "No priors, Yale graduate, works in his father's company. The family is in good standing. Mother is deceased. There isn't much more to tell. Reed has his face so he's doing his....thing."

"Thing?" Alice asked.

"Any ties to the baby case or the families?" Landon interrupted.

"No ties that I've found yet. Edward is an only child. His parents were married twenty-five years before his mom died. Prominent people. Dad is a judge and his mom was on the board of every charity event I've ever heard of, and some I haven't."

"Thanks for your help. We're just pulling up to the house. Thanks for checking."

"It's better to be safe than sorry."

"Copy that." He disconnected the call and killed the ignition.

Ten minutes later, Alice's head hit the pillow and she was settling in for a quick nap when her cell phone rang.

She answered without checking the caller ID. The only people who had access to the number were the staff at the hospital, Landon, Reed, Avery, and her sister.

"Hello."

"Alice Page?" a deep voice questioned in a voice that sounded oddly strange like a computer.

"Who is this?"

"Let me talk to Landon Love."

Alice slid out of the bed. "Not until you tell me who you are."

Alice jogged down the stairs, finding Landon in the kitchen. He turned, his gaze questioning. She pointed to the phone, and Landon flew into action, firing off a text.

"Tell me who you are and I'll let you speak to him," she demanded as Landon took her phone and hit the Speaker button

"Who is this?" Landon demanded.

"Impressive alarm." The male voice was computerized, as if trying to disguise his voice.

Every fiber in Alice's body shot to attention as she met Landon's startled gaze. His brows dipped as he turned his stare to the phone and his grip tightened. "Who is this?"

"Who I am isn't important. Not yet."

"Listen, asshole—"

"I'm the asshole that sent her the drive. I'm the asshole that breached your precious security. And I'm the asshole that knows exactly who she is."

Unease shivered down her spine.

"I'm listening. If you sent her the thumb drive, then you already have all the answers. What do you want?"

Alice raised her hand to her chest and held her breath, afraid the sound of blood rushing through her ears, combined with the sound of her breathing, would make her miss his answer. Whoever he was.

"I do have all the answers." The man paused. "A price has been put on Alice's head. Do I have your attention now?"

"Yes."

Landon's phone beeped and he glanced down at the screen before showing it to Alice. *Keep him on the phone; we're closing in on his location.*

"The men who ran the baby ring are much bigger than you could ever imagine."

"Bigger than the mafia, or the politicians that were involved?"

"They are small potatoes compared to the men running the show, and unlucky for you, they've targeted Alice. I'll be in touch, Mr. Love."

"Wait—"

The phone clicked, leaving Landon with a blank screen. He handed the phone back to Alice and dialed Avery, leaving her on speaker. "Tell me Reed traced this son of a bitch."

"We got his GPS and phone number. Reed is tracking him down as we speak."

"Thank God." Landon ran his hand over his face.

Alice released the breath she'd been holding, and the tension in her shoulders eased, if only by a margin.

"Wait....he's on the island." Avery's voice hardened. "Holy crap, honey, where did the blinking red dot just go? I need to go find this asshole so I can kick his ass."

"Baby, I can't make this guy turn his phone back on," Reed answered.

"We need to double the team on her," Landon barked while pacing the floor, tension thick in his voice.

She should be scared. After all, someone not only knew who she was, but also knew where she was. This guy had sent her information that had put a hit on her, but it didn't explain how he knew her past, or how he knew about a potential hit, or how he knew where she was hiding. What was his agenda? What did he want? Those were the questions she wanted answered. It was inevitable someone was coming for her. There was no changing that. The breakfast in her stomach sat like an unmoving brick. There was no way out of her situation, no quick fixes, and no amount of hideouts that could keep her safe.

"We need answers." Her voice came out a whisper while Landon and Avery discussed the additional security and their possible removal from the island. "We need answers," she said with more resolve, finding her voice.

Landon and Avery's plotting stopped. Landon was staring at her as if she'd grown a second head. "I promised you that we'd get answers."

She shook her head. He didn't understand, not like she did. "This is never going to stop, even if all of the families are found. They'll still come after me." She turned her gaze to the window and the lake beyond. "They won't stop," she whispered, not caring if they heard her. "They'll never stop."

"Avery, tell Reed to get me a location. I'll call you back."

Alice tuned the conversation out, drowning it with the thoughts running wild in her mind. No amount of time would make any of this go away...ever.

"Alice." Landon turned her, and she looked up into his eyes, hoping she was masking the anger and despair; both were useless, unproductive feelings. "We'll deal with this. This isn't anything more than a speed bump, and I'm a damn good driver."

His words were foreign as a cold dread settled in her spine and spread throughout her body like a virus. It was too bad she wasn't contagious and near the people causing all this pain. She'd gladly sneeze and risk life and limb to infect the bastards.

"We play offense instead of defense. That's the only way we're going to win this. We find ground zero and annihilate them."

"Alice." Landon rubbed his palms up and down her arms. The comfort he was trying to give her was admirable, even if it did nothing to ease her chill. "We don't even know the players yet. First things first. We move you. Get you as far off the island as we can, and then we'll make a plan."

"No." Her eyes widened as she stared up at him. "This is perfect." She slid out of his arms and paced the kitchen, following the same path that Landon had paced just moments ago. "This guy knows where I am. Hell, he even knows who I'm with. I don't think he wants to hurt me, or he would have by now."

"You don't know that." Landon grabbed her arm, stopping her in her tracks. He was right. She couldn't be 100 percent sure about the man's motives, but she wasn't dumb. It wasn't as though she was asking anyone to trust him.

"He called to warn us, Landon. Even if we can't trust him, we can trust that he knows what the hell is going on. He seems to be the only one who does."

"We don't even know who he is." Landon's voice grew in agitation as he moved to the French doors and rested his hands on his hip. She'd never be able to convince Landon to try and understand. It wasn't the rest of *his* life that was on the line; it was hers.

"He went to great lengths to give me the information about the babies. And following me here of all places. We're looking for a man with means and motive. That shouldn't be so hard. We figure out what he has to gain by giving me the information and tracking us and then we figure out who the hell he is."

Landon spun to face her. "And how do you propose we do that? Place an ad in the paper?"

Alice grinned. "I was thinking more like an interview on television, but an ad might work since we know he's here. This guy said he knows who I really am. Don't you want to know who I really am? I sure as hell do. I *need* to know what my part is in this twisted game."

"I know who you are. You're Alice Page. An exceptional doctor, a tinkering engineer, and the woman who is trying to get herself killed."

She gave a small shake of her head. "I need answers, Landon. We all do if we're going to stop this."

Chapter 8

After an exhausting hour arguing with Landon, Alice went to her bedroom and closed the door. Her reasoning was sound, even if her execution needed some work. They needed a plan, and not just any plan would do. They needed a way to draw this guy out while staying inconspicuous to the would-be killers that might be on their way. Landon was right about one thing. It was time to leave the tropical paradise she was growing accustomed to.

Wind rattled the shutters on the house, and she moved across the room to pull the curtains closed. She glanced down at the tree line. A man stood near one of the large trunks. Her breath hitched and she blinked several times making sure her mind wasn't playing tricks on her. She closed her eyes and opened them again. Nope, he was still there and he was watching her. He pulled something out of his pocket and held it to his ear. Within seconds, her phone vibrated in her pocket. She pulled it out, answering it without taking her eyes off the man below. She knew it was him.

"Hello," she snapped with the frustration building in her body.

"We'll meet tomorrow, Alice. You look tired. Get some sleep. No one will get close enough to harm you tonight." He lifted a purple flower into the air and crouched to set down against the trunk of the tree.

"Edward—"

"I'm impressed." She was met with silence. She glanced at her screen and when she looked back out the window to where the man was standing, the space was empty.

Alice held the phone to her chest, replaying his words in her mind. The purple flower, the man from the hospital, and the car that had followed them. Edward Best was the man who had the answers. With a heavy sigh, she turned and headed back downstairs one more time to tell Landon. Maybe after she met the guy, her need to flee might disappear as quickly as he'd done in the forest.

****

As expected, Landon reacted exactly as she'd thought, although this time he'd called in reinforcements. Avery and Reed appeared fifteen minutes later, calling out their sign that the coast was clear on the intercom so she could leave the safe room where Landon insisted she stay.

Alice jogged down the stairs and came up short when she found Landon's brother, Declan, standing in the living room, a holster with two guns strapped around his shoulder and his sheriff's badge attached to his belt.

"Any luck?" she asked, glancing around the determined faces. "Was he still out there?"

"Did he threaten you?" Declan asked.

Alice shook her head. "No. He said I looked tired and that we'd meet tomorrow."

Declan, Avery, and Landon shared a concerned glance.

Alice stepped into the living room. Her arms hugged her waist. "He said I was safe tonight. That no one would get close enough to harm me."

Declan's brows dipped as he turned to Landon. "Are you sure this guy is a foe? Everything you've told me indicates that he's trying to help. Did he do anything I can charge him with?"

"You can pick him up for trespassing," Avery answered.

"You got proof? Was he on your security feed?"

Avery and Landon exchanged a worried look. Avery hesitated before answering. "He's not on the feed."

Declan ran his hand over his face.

Landon rested his palms on his waist and lowered his head. "Alice, pack your bag. We're leaving."

"But—"

Landon's gaze shot to hers, his face stone and the mask he wore only when he was angry stared back at her. "No buts...." He gestured with his head to the stairs.

Avery rose from her seat. "I'll go start packing."

"You aren't going." Landon glanced over his shoulder. "Reed and you have a wedding to plan."

"You aren't doing this by yourself." Avery leveled him with a glare.

"Avery." Landon crossed the room and rubbed his palms up and down her arms. "Reed and you have a wedding to plan. I can't ask Reed or you to come with us. I'll call in other agents to help. You do your thing and keep Reed and the family safe. I'll take care of Alice."

"You're leaving?" Declan's voice

lowered. "That's going to kill Mom."

"We can't stay, Dec. Not without knowing the threat that's potentially coming."

Declan lowered his head and shook it. "Bring her down to the station in the morning. Give me time to find him and I'll have him picked up for questioning. At least find out what you're dealing with so you can make an informed decision before you go running off again. God only knows when you'll come back. Just let me help you this once."

"You don't have to do that."

"Of course I do. I'm your big brother."

Alice lifted her hand to her chest and held her breath. Even if Landon didn't recognize the gesture, she did. She might not have known Declan long, but in that one small gesture, she knew this was his way of trying to mend fences. Alice couldn't ask Landon to leave, not when he was close to getting his family back. She wouldn't strip him of that. She couldn't. "Let him try, Landon."

"Declan, you said yourself you have nothing to charge him with."

"Yes, I do." Declan's eyes narrowed. "Potentially breaking my mother's heart."

"I don't think that will stand up in court," Alice mumbled.

"I don't need it to." He glanced over at her. "I just need a reason to question him.

This island isn't big enough for him to hide from me."

Declan stomped over to the table and picked up the purple flower before he stomped out the front door.

Chapter 9

The moment they were alone, Alice stood in front of him looking up into his eyes. "Stubbornness runs in your family, doesn't it?"

"You could say that," Landon mumbled.

Alice gave a knowing nod and then reached for Landon and hugged his waist. He might not realize he needed the hug, but right now, she did.

Landon's arms were slow to wrap around her. His hard body was unyielding. She didn't care. She squeezed him tighter and laid her head on his chest. How long had it been since he let someone get close?

"This is where you're supposed to hug me back," she whispered.

His body shook in a silent chuckle. "Is that so?"

"Yeah, that's so." She smiled against his chest.

A second later, his arms wrapped around her. His fingers ran a soothing motion over her back.

"Alice, I know you want to stay...but it's not safe."

"I know." Her words came out a whisper. "I'll call the hospital and make arrangements. Knowing someone is coming to kill me kind of puts things in perspective. I don't want any of my patients to get caught in the crossfire."

Landon's fingers trailed a slow path up her back and sifted into her hair. "Always thinking of others"—he smiled and leaned back to look down at her— "when you're the one in danger. That's who you are, Alice. No matter what we find."

She gave a small smile, knowing his words were meant to comfort her. He pressed his lips into her hair. Her heart raced in hopes that he'd kiss her anywhere but there. "Get packed and then try and get some rest."

"We're leaving regardless of whether or not your brother finds Edward, aren't we?"

"They should have never picked this place for me to protect you."

Right. How could she forget? He was being forced to be there, to spend time with her to keep her safe. Her heart clenched, and her body deflated. His words weren't meant to hurt her…yet the truth remained. She was his job.

Alice dropped her hold and took a tentative step back. First one and then two. "I'm so sorry, Landon. I didn't mean to do this to you."

"Alice, you didn't do anything." He started to close the distance between them, and she held up her hand, stilling him.

"Landon, I'm tired. I'm just going to pack and try to get some sleep." She gestured with her thumb toward the stairs.

He didn't try and stop her, not that she gave him a chance. She jogged up the stairs and stepped into her room. Shutting her door, she leaned back against the wood and closed her eyes. She had to leave, but that didn't mean Landon had to go with her. She'd ask to be reassigned, hoping he stayed on the island. Maybe, just maybe, she could lead the danger away from his door, away from his island, and away from him.

Alice took a shower and changed into a pair of shorts and tank top to wear to bed.

Grabbing her toiletries, she dropped them into one of her bags and began pulling clothes out of the closet and the dressers and shoved those in her suitcase, leaving out one change of clothes she'd wear in the morning. She turned off the light and moved to the window, staring outside at the beauty the island had to offer. All that promise she'd yet to explore. Her gaze moved to the spot where she'd seen Edward. A shiver skirted down her spine as she remembered his words. Bigger fish and a contract on her head. Her time was limited. She could hear it in Edward's voice, and she knew it in her heart. Her world had crumbled in a matter of a month into the tatters of something unrecognizable.

She heard the light knock and the creak of her door opening and turned just as Landon stood under the threshold. His gaze scanned the bed before it landed on her. "I thought you were asleep."

She shook her head and turned back to the window. "I can't sleep. I was trying to memorize how beautiful it is here."

Landon stepped into the room and moved over to her, repositioning her to the side of the windowsill. "You shouldn't be near the window. He might still be out there."

Alice rested her back against the wall. "Do you know what I realized from all of this?”

Landon remained quiet, his gaze assessing. Could he tell she’d cried in the shower? Was there evidence in her face, in her voice?

“A future is a luxury that I don’t have. It was stripped away from me the day I got the thumb drive.”

She gave him a brave smile, even though her heart was cracking into a million pieces. She was going to miss him. She was going to miss all of them.

“You aren’t giving up.” His words were quiet between them. He moved closer and rested his hands on her hips. “I won’t let you.”

Her brows dipped. He’d spoken as if he’d read her mind. Maybe she was shit at covering her emotions. Maybe the mask she thought she had in place had slipped.

“I’m not giving up,” she lied. “I’m being realistic.”

“I don’t believe you.” He pressed her into the wall, his body plastered against hers. His hands still gripped her sides. “Don’t do this.”

“I haven’t done anything.” She held his gaze and watched the mix of emotions cross his face.

“I know that look,” he said, lowering his head so that he could whisper in his ear. “I see it every day in the mirror. You think this is your fault.”

Alice's breath hitched. The pounding of his heart was steady and pressing against her chest. "It is my fault."

"No, baby, it's not," he whispered against her neck before he pressed a kiss to the sensitive spot. "Stop living in your head and talk to me."

Alice's heart raced a mile a minute from Landon holding her in a lover's embrace. His excitement was pressed against her belly. There was no denying the desire she could see so clearly in his eyes. The fire and heat that he felt toward her matched hers in every way. "Shut up and kiss me."

Landon's lips twitched; his fingers caressed her sides making a slow path up her torso until his thumbs rested right below her breasts. "You're demanding."

"You were warned as I recall."

"What do you want, Alice?"

Alice visibly swallowed in her hesitation. Should she dare tell him what she'd been thinking for the last month that she'd been around him?

"Tell me," he demanded.

Her eyes softened as she stared up at him. "One night, in your arms, without having to worry if someone is going to kill me."

His lips tilted at the corners as he lowered his head. His lips hovered over hers when he whispered, "Consider it done."

He kissed her like a man starved. His lips, playful at first, turned hungry and heated. His fingers slid beneath the hem of her tank top, and she thought she'd die feeling his skin against hers. He moved up her stomach gut-wrenchingly slow, heating her skin and awakening every nerve in her body. His palm cupped her breast, and he gave a gentle squeeze, rolling the nipple between his fingers.

He swallowed her moan that slipped free before he moved his lips to her neck.

"This is your last chance to back out." He pulled his lips away from their assault.

"Not on your life," she whispered and cupped his erection beneath his jeans.

His grin grew. "You and me, one night, no one killing you."

She nodded and rubbed his erection.

He cupped her ass and lifted her off her feet. She locked her legs behind his back and giggled. "Where are you taking me?"

He yanked the closet door open and punched in the numbers on the keypad. The door slid open and he stepped inside with her, not letting her feet touch the ground until the door slid closed. "You're safe in here."

The safe room was smaller than her bedroom, but not by much. It held a queen-sized bed, a small couch, a fridge, a small bathroom, and a storage area. The walls were lined with video cameras that surrounded the property, not to mention a phone on the wall that could be used even if the lines were cut.

"This is a bad idea. You know that, right?" He reached for the hem of her shirt, slid it up her body, and then dropped it to the floor.

"The worst," she breathed on a sigh as his lips found her breast. He walked her back to the bed, never breaking contact.

"I could lose my job," he countered, as if trying to talk himself out of it. He slipped his fingers inside her panties, not stopping until he found her mound. He ran his finger over her desire and she moaned again.

"I could lose my life," she countered. "I think mine trumps yours."

He slipped a finger inside, and she thought she'd come undone. She was wet and wanting, and there would be no denying it now. Ever.

"Ahh." He sighed with a smile on his lips. "So wet for me, baby."

Alice took the pleasure of slipping her shorts and thong down her legs without losing the finger he stroked her with. She needed him, and she needed more. She widened her stance, showing him exactly what she wanted.

"So demanding." He kissed her lips

again with determination. Each thrust of his tongue matched his finger. He slipped another one inside, and she held on, hoping her legs didn't give out.

Landon eased her down to sit on the bed before he dropped to his knees in front of her. Running his hands up her thighs, he kissed a trail from her lips, down her neck, and over her stomach, only stopping above her mound. He eased her legs open wider, and Alice fell back on the bed. He slipped his finger inside her slick folds and stroked her again. Her eyes were hooded as she watched him, feeling everything as if it were her first time.

"You ready, baby? I've only got one night to blow your mind until this thing is resolved."

"Better make it count." She winked.

Landon twisted his finger and found her G-spot the moment his lips descended down on her. The combination of the spot and his mouth working her sent her into a frenzy. She gripped the comforter and lifted her hips to give him better access, and within minutes, she felt the tightening of her walls, and her toes curled to stave off the pressure. She didn't want her release to be so quick. She wanted to savor every moment. She held on, fighting against what she knew would be the hardest orgasm she'd ever had.

"Give it to me, Alice."

She shook her head, and he continued his torture.

"Baby, you're so tight. I can't wait to be inside you, to feel your sheath sucking me in."

She couldn't hold it any longer. His words, coupled with his tongue and his finger, pushed her over the edge into full-blown sensation. She screamed his name as she dug her nails into the covers, afraid if she let go she would float away.

Landon slowed his movements as she came down from her high. He kissed her once more between her thighs before he rose to stand in front of her.

Pulling out his wallet, he took a condom out and tossed it on the bed. He held her gaze as he pulled his shirt above his head and dropped it to the floor. Landon was amazing. His abs were riddled with tiny scars she could only assume were from his time in the military. His toned body held a promise, and she couldn't wait to touch. She sat up and lifted her hand to his chest, running her fingers over his muscles. Her gaze zeroed in on his fingers working the button on his jeans. The sound of the zipper going down gave her a fresh wave of wetness between her thighs.

He pushed his jeans down and kicked them off. He was commando all right. His erection sprang forth, his girth and length teasing her with the promise of pleasure she'd yet to experience.

Alice held on to his thighs and leaned in for a taste. She licked the head teasingly before she took him into her mouth. Landon's hand shot into her hair, holding her in a grip.

He moaned. "Damn, Alice."

His words spurred her on, and she started moving, her tongue gliding along the smooth surface. She sucked him, trying to give him back the pleasure he'd given her.

"Fuck." He groaned while slipping his cock deeper into her mouth before he pulled free. "I need to be in you, Alice."

He slid up her body, easing her back to the middle of the mattress. He sat back on his thighs and rolled the condom down his shaft, never taking his intense gaze off her. He leaned down and positioned himself between her thighs, and without another word, he pushed home, sending them both into a world where they spent hours in nothing but pleasure and ecstasy.

Chapter 10

They lay in a heap of tangled limbs on the bed. Every muscle in his body was sated, and he figured hers were too. Sex, he told himself. That was all it was. A way to relieve the stress he could see in her eyes, and what he'd been feeling himself. Alice rested her head against his chest and her hand traced the lines on his stomach. The latest were thanks to a knife fight with someone who'd been close to outmaneuvering him.

"Did you get all these in the military?" she asked, lifting up and placing a gentle kiss over the scar.

"Not all of them, but most," he answered. His gaze moved to the monitors hanging on the wall. He scanned them like he'd done several times into the early morning hours.

"Landon…when this is over—"

He didn't let her finish what she was going to say. Instead, he rolled her onto her back and kissed her with the force of the emotions he felt wafting from her. "When this is over, I want to take you on a date."

She laughed for the first time since he'd known her. "A date?"

He nodded and kissed the freckle on her neck. "Yep. You and me…we'll go on a date like a real couple."

She smiled, her eyes lit like emeralds. "You've got yourself a deal." She glanced at the monitor and her emerald eyes widened. "Did you see that?"

Landon kissed her lips one last time and rolled off of her. "See what, baby?"

"I saw something….someone…movement."

Landon propped himself up and studied the screens. "Was it an animal or a person?"

Her eyes widened in terror as she watched three men converging on the house. Landon and she were safe behind the steel walls; she knew that, but her heart didn't get the memo and threatened to beat out of her chest. "Are those guns?"

"Fuck," Landon said, jumping to his feet and grabbing his jeans.

Alice grabbed his arm to stop him. "Landon, no. You can't take them all."

"Get dressed," he barked and lifted the phone on the wall and started punching in numbers. "We've got a strike team coming in from the east."

He hung up, looked around the small room, grabbed his gun, and shoved it in his jeans while they watched the images on the screen. The flash of red from the machine guns came in quick succession. One was aimed at the entire lower floor and the other up to the second when they noticed two more men at the front of the house. The shooters opened fire, as Landon and Alice watched the unimaginable happen.

Landon moved to the phone, picked it up, and punched in more numbers. "We've got five, armed with machine guns, Avery. Alice and I are in the safe room. Hold your position and call for backup. Do. Not. Approach. On your own."

"I'm calling in help. Shoot anyone who breaches the safe room door."

"Copy that." He hung up.

Landon tossed Alice her clothes and moved her to the far wall before tipping the bed to hide her from sight. He flipped on the intercom system and stood with his gun pointed at the door, his finger on the trigger. The sound of glass shattering filled the room, matching the sound of bullets that were raining in the house.

Alice had her head poked out from behind the mattress, and she watched the monitors. They both did. Rain poured down, and Landon knew instantly who Avery had called. There was only one relative that could bring the rain, not to mention the lightning. He watched, his gaze intent on the black figures that were now highlighted in the thunder and lightning. A calming ease swept down his spine and he whispered, “Alexis.”

“Who?”

“My cousin. Avery called my cousin, Alexis.”

“Is she some commando too?”

Landon chuckled. “Worse. A pissed-off beautician.” Landon glanced over his shoulder. “You don’t want to watch this in case she misses and actually strikes one of these guys.”

Alice rose to her feet and watched as the lightning struck and danced around the men outside, the gunfire forgotten. First one and then three men took off for the cover of the trees, lightning striking the ground behind them as they ran. “How…”

Landon realized his mistake the

minute she asked. He'd never told Alice about his family or his cousins. He'd never trusted her enough to tell her the truth, unsure if their assignment was temporary.

Landon debated his reply, taking a moment to form the right words and watching the monitor as the other two guys scrambled away. He lowered his gun and turned to face Alice. "This is going to be kind of hard to explain."

"Try me." Her eyes danced between him and the screen and the way the lightning moved away from the house.

"You know how your DNA is in question? Well, mine isn't, and neither is that of my cousins. Each of us has, rather all of us have, an ability that we can't explain. My cousin"—he pointed to the monitor—"can control the weather...to some extent," he amended.

Alice gave a slow nod. "And you?"

"I can feel emotions."

"That's how you knew I was about to throw in the towel."

Landon nodded.

"Declan? What's his?"

"He's like a human lie detector."

Alice leaned against the wall, as if her legs were about to give out.

"Skylar?"

"She's got this aura thing going on. She can see lights around everyone."

Alice gave a slow nod, as if still

needing time to process it all.

"What about Flynn? Him too?"

"Premonitions."

Alice's mouth parted for a mere second before she snapped it closed. "And when Avery said that Reed was doing his thing with Edward's picture? What thing might that be?"

"Well, you already know that Reed is a computer geek. There's a reason he's so good. If it's online, or in electronic format, he can access it, no matter what secrets the individual is trying to hide."

Her face reddened, and her eyes narrowed. "Were you ever going to tell me?"

"Not unless there was a need," Landon answered instantly. "There wasn't until now."

She gave a slow nod and snapped her mouth closed as she stepped around the mattress. "You can sleep with me; you can be intimate with every part of my body, but you don't trust me enough to tell me something so... so... important."

"Alice, not many people know. Could you imagine if they did? We'd be studied and experimented on. I couldn't do that to my family. I'd never intentionally put them in harm's way."

"Like bringing me to the island?"

The phone on the wall rang, interrupting their conversation, and

Landon hesitated answering it. Keeping Alice pegged with his gaze, he picked it up. "Yeah."

"They should be gone," Avery announced.

"They are. Tell Alexis thanks for me."

"I'm pulling in. Holy...moly...the house looks like Swiss cheese."

"It's safe to say that it's compromised. Use the intercom after your sweep and let us know it's clear."

"Copy that."

Landon hung up and shoved the gun into the waistband of his jeans. He stepped toward Alice. "Baby, I'm sorry."

All the blood drained from Alice's face. She closed her eyes and dropped her gaze to her feet. "Anything else you've kept secret? Is Avery some superhero spy?"

Landon tried to cover his smile and failed miserably. "If you ask her, she is, but not from her DNA."

"Surf's up," came over the speaker.

Landon punched the numbers on the panel and stepped out of the room, finding Avery waiting in Alice's room. She was zipping up Alice's suitcase and moving it to the door.

"I suggest you get your stuff."

"Do you think it was Edward Best?" Landon asked on his way to the door.

"No," Alice answered. "He told me I would be safe tonight."

"Or he gave up our location," Landon said.

"I'm afraid she's right, Landon. It wasn't Best."

Landon stopped at the door. "How do you know?"

"He was picked up within an hour of Declan leaving here. Declan has had him this entire time, trying to get him to talk. He said he'd only talk to Alice and that the police were keeping him from stopping an attack. I guess we know he was telling the truth now."

"Give me five." Landon left them to go into his room and grab his things, which he'd already packed. He moved to the holes in the wall plaster and glanced back at his bed. The stuffing and springs were sticking out of it, and it was in that moment that he knew he'd escaped death. "Fuck me."

"Get your ass in gear, Love. We'll be downstairs."

Landon grabbed his duffel bag from the closet, hefted it over his shoulder, and trampled down the stairs to find Avery and Alice standing by the door waiting. Avery tossed him the keys to his SUV.

The first floor of the house was worse than the second story. Glass was shattered everywhere. Furniture was filled with bullets and holes, as was the drywall. Landon's muscles tensed and his jaw ticked. They'd gotten close to Alice. Too close.

Anger radiated from him, filling the air and mixing with the apprehension that Alice was giving off. This wasn't happening again. Ever.

Landon followed the girls to the vehicles. Alice got into Avery's car without giving him a second glance. Landon stood with the driver's side door open when Avery lifted her shoulders.

"Where to?" he asked.

"Showers first. You both smell like sex. And then the police station. You've got your choice of shacking up with Reed and me or at your parents' cabin."

"Reed and you," Alice answered for them.

"I guess we'll be staying with Reed and you."

Avery left the car door open and walked around to stand in front of Landon.

"I don't know what happened between you two, and I don't care, but you need to fix this." Her brows rose in challenge.

"I had to tell her about us."

"Oh."

"All of us. I slipped up and mentioned Alexis causing the lightning."

"Well, that explains it." She patted Landon on the arm. "We're driving slowly, so I can undo your damage."

"Thanks."

"Don't thank me yet. If this is about your abilities, then I've got you covered. If it has anything to do with the monkey sex I smell on you guys, then you're on your own."

Chapter 11

Landon glanced toward Alice in the passenger seat for a second time. They'd both showered and changed. Separately. And she'd had time to absorb Avery's explanation as to why she'd been left in the dark. It made sense, even if she felt like a fool. After spending a month with Landon, she'd thought she knew him. She knew his moods as if they were married. She'd met his family. Hell, she even knew the way he worked tactical maneuvers. She just hadn't been privy to the family secret. She'd slept with a man she wasn't sure she knew anything about, and even worse, she'd been the one to instigate it. She couldn't be mad at him for that. Could she?

Landon turned in the opposite direction of the police station, and Alice glanced out the back window. "I thought it was that way."

"It is." He kept driving. "We're making a pit stop first."

"For what?" she asked. "Ice cream?"

Landon's lips twitched. "Not exactly, but we can get you some if you're hungry."

Alice didn't ask any more questions since it was evident Landon wasn't the type of person to share. She didn't say a word when he turned off the main road and parked the SUV, or when he came around to her side and held out his hand. No, she didn't say a word when he slipped his fingers through hers and led her down a steep, sandy path to what she believed was the beach.

She was right. They stepped out onto the beach and he moved her in front of him, wrapping his arms around her waist.

"What are we doing here?"

"This is my favorite spot in the world, and I wanted to share it with you."

"Oh, now you want to share," she teased, or was she?

"I've been all over the world, and I've never been able to duplicate this."

"What?" she asked, unsure what to expect.

The sun started to rise over the horizon. The reds and yellows danced on the ocean water as waves crashed along the shore. It was a beach, just like the others she'd seen. Why this one was special she either didn't have a clue or hadn't spotted the difference, so she waited. Birds flew in the air, swooping down to get their breakfast from the sea.

Landon leaned into her ear. "Wait for it..."

She glanced around, hoping she wasn't missing some spectacular show, and she felt something land softly on her head. She reached up and grabbed it, bringing it to eye level. A white petal from a flower. Within seconds, there were thousands flying over their heads, landing on them, the beach, and in the water.

"How?" she asked, reaching down to pick up one of the full flowers.

"My cousin, Alexis," he answered and hugged her tighter. "She jogs this route every morning, and every time she does, the breeze blows and the petals drift down from above. It brings new meaning to the word sun shower."

Alice couldn't contain her smile as she watched the thousands of petals dance in the sky. "This is beautiful."

Landon rested his head on her

shoulder, and they both gazed out at the sun and the flowers. "This is where I find my peace. The sunrise, the flowers, the breeze, and the water. This is my heaven, and now you're a part of it."

Landon turned her in his arms and held her waist. "I may not always know the right thing to say, or trust people easily, but I want you to know that I trust you, and when I'm with you, there is no place I'd rather be."

"Landon…"

He leaned down and pressed his lips to hers in a gentle kiss. "I enjoyed every minute we were in the safe room."

"Up until the bullets started flying?"

"Yeah, up until then. Alice, I'm not going to lie. We're both lucky to be alive, and we probably wouldn't be if we hadn't been in that room. I'm not sure you're safe with me anymore. I can't seem to focus when you're next to me, or in the room, and that's no way to ensure your safety."

"Are you saying you don't want to protect me?"

"I'm saying I'd die to protect you, Alice. I'm just not sure I'm suited to run your operation. Not in the way you need. I want you safe, and I almost lost you last night. I. Can't. Lose. You. Too."

"You won't." Alice lifted her palm to his face. "We'll figure this out." She leaned up on her tiptoes and pressed a kiss to his lips. “I trust you.”

“You might come to regret that,” he teased and took her hand, leading her back to the SUV.

Fifteen minutes later, Alice was laughing as she picked the flower petals out of her hair while they walked into the police station. All work had stopped before the door swung closed behind them. Declan stepped out of his office, his permanent scowl planted on his face. Landon’s other brother, Flynn, walked out behind him. Alice leaned into Landon and whispered, “What did you say Flynn can do?”

“Premonitions.”

“That doesn’t sound good,” she whispered, and they kept walking.

“Any change?” Landon asked as he approached Declan.

“With Best, no,” he answered. “But there is a new development we need to talk about.”

“You can say that again.” Flynn clapped Landon on the arm before plucking a flower petal from Alice’s hair. “Crap.” He shook his head, and his eyes softened as he stared at Alice. “I’m sorry, darling. I wanted to be wrong.” He held up the petal “But it looks like I’m right again.”

“Right about what?” Landon asked, knocking the petal from his hand. “Start talking.”

“Not here.” Flynn started walking to the interrogation room. He held out his hand, waited for them all to enter, and then called out to one of the other deputies. “Give us ten minutes and then bring him in.”

Flynn shut the door and leaned against the wood. “I don’t know how to tell you this.” His gaze met Landon’s.

“Just spill it. I already told her about all of us. There are no more secrets.”

“In thirty minutes, when you two leave, there will be a gunman waiting outside. There is going to be bloodshed.”

“Whose?” Declan asked, his arms crossed over his chest.

“Alice’s and Landon’s,” Flynn answered. “She’s going to take two to the chest, and he’s going to take one in the arm.”

“We’ll take them out the back,” Declan declared and moved to shove Flynn out of the way.

“I’ve seen that scenario, too. There’s more than one gunman, in case the other fails.”

“Let me guess. There are five?” Landon asked.

Flynn grinned. “Are you honing in on my premonitions?”

“That’s how many shot up the safe house,” Alice answered. Declan and Flynn swung their gazes to her.

"Focus," Landon said. "Is there a scenario where we get her out alive?"

"Funny you should ask that. Yes, but you are definitely not going to like it."

"Well?" Landon asked impatiently.

"She has to leave with Best." He held up his hand. "Specifically, she has to have a gun pointed at his head and they won't shoot her. Any other way, and she dies."

Landon sent a chair from the table careening across the room. "Absolutely fucking not."

"Landon." Alice linked her hand with his, needing the grounding and his strength. She turned back to the brothers. "What is so special about this guy?"

"I have no clue," Flynn answered.

"I don't know either," Declan said. "Since I assume you know I'm a lie detector, it's hard to determine the truth and a lie if the asshole won't talk to me."

"But he'll talk to me?" she asked.

"No," Landon growled. "That's not happening."

Alice turned to Landon and her face softened. "It's the only way." She turned back to Flynn. "How does Landon get out of here safely?"

"He has to leave with me in the next five minutes. Anything longer and we're toast as well."

"Then we'll take her with us." Landon started heading for the door.

"They see her and we're all dead. She's the trigger. Once the man in the front moves to the back, in the next four minutes, they'll shoot you too. Right now the guy out back doesn't know that you two came together. They won't suspect anything when we leave."

"Are you kidding me?" Landon asked incredulously. "There has to be another way."

"There's not, Lan. I'm sorry," Flynn answered. "You need to tell her goodbye now so we can leave.

Alice turned to him and grabbed his face, pressing a hard kiss to his lips. "Go. I'll reach out to you. I promise."

His eyes pleaded with her, and she could barely hold back the tears. "Go. Now." She pushed him toward Flynn, who grabbed his arm and started pulling him toward the door. "Go."

Landon cursed the entire way down the hall with Flynn dragging him to the door.

Alice paced to the other side of the room and stopped. She swiped at a tear that slipped free. "I can lock you in the basement and we can shoot anyone who comes for you."

Alice shook her head and turned. "I need this to stop, and Best seems to be the only one holding the cards. I can't let anyone else get hurt because of me."

Declan stepped closer to her, pulled her into his arms, and hugged her. "You don't worry about us. I've got *us* covered." He leaned back and looked down into her eyes. "You worry about you. You keep yourself safe, and Landon will come for you. I know it like I know I'd go after Olivia. He'll come for you, trust that."

"Declan—"

"No matter what he says, you look at me. I'll nod yes if he's telling the truth and shake my head no if he's lying. Okay?"

She nodded at the same time the door behind them opened. In walked a deputy with Best wearing a bulletproof vest and his hands cuffed in front of him. A female deputy followed him, carrying a bulletproof vest. She moved to Alice and helped her get into it.

"That's unnecessary. I'm not going to hurt her, and I don't have a weapon," Best said.

Alice glanced at Declan, and he gave a little nod to let her know that Best was telling the truth.

Declan made a motion to have Best's cuffs removed, and he gestured toward the chair. "Sit."

Best complied.

"How do you know me?" Alice asked.

"I thought your first question would be why I sent you the thumb drive," he answered, evading her question.

"I know why you sent the thumb drive. I'm one of the stolen children. Now answer my question. How do you know me?"

He remained quiet, and Declan checked his watch. "Answer her question. You two are running out of time."

"Time for what?" Best asked, glancing between them both.

"Answer her damn question," Declan growled while removing the gun from his leg holster. He handed it to Alice.

Best's brows dipped as he watched the exchange. "Let's just say we're related."

Alice glanced at Declan, and he nodded. Damn. "How are we related?"

"You aren't safe here, Alice. I need to get you off the island."

Declan nodded again. "Assuming I leave with you, how do you plan to get me off the Island?"

"My helicopter. I've been here since the day you stepped foot on the Island."

Declan nodded again.

The thought of flying made her stomach roll.

"Where would you take her?"

"Someplace these thugs would be killed if they step foot."

"Where!" Declan slammed his hand down on the table.

"My home. 514 Brighton Rd. in Sweeton, Pennsylvania."

"Fine." Declan pulled out his phone

and started typing a text.

"Landon Love will be meeting us at your house, and if you so much as harm a hair on his body, I'll destroy you," Alice said with more ferocity than she'd ever said anything before.

"Count on it," Declan replied.

Best leaned back in his chair with a smirk on his face. "How do you plan to do that?"

"You seem like a smart guy to me. I knew that from the way the file was encrypted. First I'll start with your bank accounts then move to your credit cards, and if that's not enough, then probably your trust fund. I bet you're a trust fund baby. Your daddy, the judge, would have set something like that up for you since you work for him." Alice paced the floor. "Then I think we'll move to daddy's company." She stopped and turned toward him. "Or how about I have it leaked to the press that you were the one who supplied me with the data. I'm sure the assholes that tried to gun me down last night wouldn't mind the extra hit."

"Feisty. The apple doesn't fall very far from the tree. I shouldn't be surprised." His playful look turned serious. "They tried to kill you last night?" Edward's nostrils flared, and he turned his glare toward Declan. "I warned you, if you didn't let me go, she was as good as dead."

"And I'm warning you, if Landon or she gets hurt, *you're* as good as dead."

"Your boyfriend and you are welcome in my home, and I will guarantee your safety as long as you stay on my compound."

Alice glanced at Declan. He nodded.

"Why would you do that?" She asked.

"I'll explain when we get there."

"Perfect." She rounded the table and gestured for Best to stand. She glanced up at Declan. "How are we doing this?"

He pulled the keys out of his pocket and tossed them to her. "You're taking my SUV. It's been pulled up to the back exit. The door is unlocked, and it's bulletproof, which will give you some cover. Keep your head down and get into it as fast as you can. I have men positioned to try and hold the shooters off as long as possible. Landon is going to meet you at the helicopter."

"They're here?" Edward asked and glanced at her. "You can't leave. They have orders to kill on sight."

"I'll take my chances." With gun in hand, she ushered him out of the conference room. She handed him the keys and paused in front of the exit door. Declan was standing behind them.

"The safety is on, so don't worry about the trigger. You won't accidently blow his head off."

Declan pointed to the switch and showed her how to flick it.

Chapter 12

Alice leaned into Best. “I trusted you last night when you said I’d be safe.”

“If the law wouldn’t have picked me up, you would have been safe.”

“Ready?”

She glanced back at Declan. “Clear the hall so no one accidently gets shot, just in case these jerks actually fire at me.”

Declan barked an order down the hallway and it immediately cleared.

“You too,” she whispered and used the gun to gesture to the side room.

His brows dipped. He didn't like being told what to do, but at least, he'd be alive to bitch about it later.

Alice positioned the gun to Edward's head and took a deep breath. "If we make it out of this alive, I want answers."

He gave a quick nod. "I'll do my best."

Alice yanked the door open without any hesitation. She held the gun pressed to Edward's head and ducked, keeping them both low. Shots rang out in the air, but not at either Edward or her as they climbed into the SUV.

Gunfire exploded around them in different directions, all aimed into the woods. Edward pressed the gas pedal to the floor and had the tires squealing as they sped away. Alice kept glancing out the back window and let out a little sigh when no one was quick to follow.

The air in the SUV was filled with tension, and she tried to cover the shake in her hands as they sped toward the private airport. The guard gate was open and the guard gone when they pulled in. The hanger was open. Landon had the helicopter out and was sitting in the pilot seat. The copter door was open, waiting for them to climb in. She breathed her first sigh of relief that he would be going with her and she wouldn't have to wait for him to show up.

Alice shoved the car door open;

Edward dropped the keys on the seat of the SUV and hurried with her to the helicopter, yanking the doors closed after they both climbed in.

Edward climbed up into the co-pilot seat before he spoke. “Go, go, go.”

The blades swished to life, and within minutes, they were hovering up into the air and leaving the Island behind. Edward held out his headset so Alice could see what he was doing. He slid it over his ears, and she grabbed the pair hanging next to her. “Do you know where you’re going?”

“Yep.” Landon glanced back to meet Alice’s gaze. “Are you okay?”

She nodded and held up her thumb. “A little shaken but bullet free.”

“Bullet free is good.” He winked and turned back around.

“If we get out of this alive, remind me to personally thank your family.”

“You’ll get out unscathed, Alice. Now that you’ve been seen with me, no one will make another hit on your life. The message has been sent.”

“And what message would that be?” Landon asked and exchanged a quick glance with Edward.

“The message that there is no secret that has been left hidden.” He smiled. “I’ll explain everything when we land.”

Thirty minutes later, they were descending into an open field next to a mansion. Her stomach rolled and she felt faint. She'd closed her eyes for most of the flight, afraid that if she looked down she might toss her cookies.

"You live here?" Alice asked.

"Welcome to my home, Alice. You are welcome here anytime and under any circumstances."

Alice could see only the side of Landon's face, but she didn't miss the way his jaw hardened at Edward's words. Landon landed the helicopter and powered down. He was quick to exit and yank the back door open. He held out his arms to her, and she flew into his embrace. He kissed her hard before letting her feet hit the ground.

"I thought I'd lost you."

"Not a chance," she whispered back as Edward got out.

"Do you want answers, or do you want to stay out here all day playing kissy face with the commando?"

She grinned. "Kissy face sounds nice."

"Answers now, kissy face later." Landon winked and kissed her again.

Alice handed Declan's gun to Landon, glad that she wasn't responsible for it anymore. He stashed it in his waistband and took her hand, and they followed Edward into the humongous house.

Security guards were stationed around the perimeter, wearing suits and carrying machine guns. Another man in a suit met Edward at the back door. He was in his early forties and sported a short cropped cut. He exchanged some words with Edward before making his way to Landon. A smile stretched across his face. "Love, well I'll be damned."

"Maverick Jones? What the hell are you doing here?"

"I could ask you the same thing," he answered, and they all walked into the house.

"Good, you two know each other. That will make things easier, "What would like to drink, Alice? Wine, beer, whatever you want. If I don't have it, I'll get it. I think you're going to need some alcohol for the conversation we're about to have."

"Beer is fine," she answered as she glanced among the men. "I'm sure Maverick and Landon knowing each other wasn't a coincidence."

"Smart and feisty." Edward grinned. "It runs in our DNA."

Edward moved to the fridge, pulled out four bottles of beer, handing her one before offering the others to Landon and Maverick. Landon waived off the alcohol and Edward shrugged before popping the top on his own.

"Yeah, and exactly whose DNA would that be?" she asked, taking a swig of her beer. Landon wrapped an arm around her waist and kept her pulled against his back.

"The parent we share," he answered, and Alice was sure her mouth hung open as she stared at the man, sure he was delusional. Her legs turned to noodles, and without Landon's arm, she would have fallen on her ass.

"Excuse me?" she asked.

"I'm your half brother," he answered without any more elaboration. "Whoa, I've been waiting years to say that out loud." He grinned. "This will be easier in the study, where I can show you how I found you."

They followed Edward out of the kitchen and into a huge room off the main area. He held out his arm to usher them in and stopped Maverick. "Can you make sure that Ellie has a room prepared for Mr. Love and my sister?"

Maverick nodded and was out of sight before Alice could sit in one of the chairs in front of the desk.

Landon stood behind Alice's seat with his hand on her shoulder. The connection wasn't lost on her. She rested her hand over his, and gave a gentle pat, acknowledging his support, and if she had to guess, he was making a tactical stance.

"Tracking down your parents would have been virtually impossible from your end." He glanced up as he pulled a file out of the drawer. "Not that I don't have faith in your abilities. I'm glad you've managed to stay alive this far. That's an impressive feat compared to what you're up against."

Edward sat in the chair and let out an audible sigh. "Lucky for both of us, I found the missing link and the information, or I would have never known about you either. They were good, but they underestimated me."

"Who?" Landon asked.

"I'm getting to that," Edward answered. "But first, I need to lay the foundation for you to appreciate the magnitude of what has happened."

Landon nodded for him to continue.

"Alice Page, you were born Lucy St. Claire on December twenty-sixth, 1986, in Charleston, West Virginia."

A gasp left her lips.

Landon squeezed her shoulder and leaned down to kiss the top of her head.

"How old are you?" she asked, unsure if the man claiming to be her brother was older or younger.

"I'm your older brother by five years." He grinned. "Exciting, isn't it?"

"I wouldn't use that word," she mumbled and then gestured toward the file. "Please continue."

"Here's the hard part of the story."

She nodded and braced herself for the inevitable. "I know I was stolen and sold.

Is there something harder than that?"

He held her gaze, his look serious. "Yes. This will be harder than that."

"Oh God," she whispered. "Just tell me like you're ripping off a Band-Aid. Don't prolong it."

"Strong too." He grinned. "As you wish." He stood and rounded the desk to sit in the chair that Landon hadn't taken. "Like I said, we're half siblings. My father, Edward Best Senior, the sleazebag that he is, cheated on my mother with your mother, Lucille St. Claire. They had an ongoing affair in which you were conceived. When Lucille found out she was pregnant, their relationship took a turn for the worse. She wanted him to leave my mother, and he refused, so being the strong woman that your mother was, she left him without any support or demands. She told him she was keeping you and he wasn't going to be a part of your life."

"Oh God," she whispered, unsure she wanted to hear any more but knowing she'd regret it if she told him to stop.

"How do you know this?" Landon asked the question she was scared to ask.

"My mother," Edward answered before turning his gaze back to Alice. "I'm getting to that." He let out a shaky breath and grabbed the file on his desk. He pulled out a picture and handed it to her. "This is your mom."

Alice's eyes watered as she stared at her spitting image, a woman who looked only a few years older. She had the same cheekbones and the same unruly hair. She was beautiful. "Where is she now?"

"She died," he answered flatly. "But I'm getting ahead of the story." Edward cleared his throat. "Your mother stayed true to her word. She didn't contact my father at all, and exactly two weeks after you were born, you were in the car with her when she was involved in a fatal car accident. You obviously survived, but she didn't."

"No one in her family went looking for me?"

"They didn't know about you. It's worse than that." He reached for her hand and squeezed. "My father hired the hit man that blew her tire and killed her. The same hit man was told that, if you survived, he was to kill you as well."

"But he didn't," she whispered. Her heart cracked into a million pieces.

"But he didn't," Edward agreed. "He brought you back to my dad and told him he wasn't a baby killer, and said if he wanted it done, to do it himself. Dad was the one who sold you to your other family."

"Oh my God." She covered her mouth with her hand. "I think I'm going to be sick."

Landon helped her to her feet. "Where's the closest bathroom?"

"Across the hall," Edward said.

Alice hurried with Landon's help into the bathroom. She tried her best to hold her hair back as she leaned over the porcelain and proceeded to empty the contents of her stomach.

Landon eased the hair out of her hands and held it for her while rubbing her back. "You're strong, Alice. We'll handle this just like we've handled everything else, baby. I'll be with you every step of the way. I promise."

"My father sold me," she said with all of the venom she could muster as she rose from the toilet. She flushed the toilet and moved to the sink. Cupping her hands under the water, she rinsed her mouth before splashing water on her face. "The fucking bastard killed my mother and sold me."

Landon turned her into his chest and wrapped his arms around her, holding her in the warmth and security his hold gave her. The fact that she needed it wasn't lost on her. Just something else to throw into the mix of the fucked-up life she was living.

"I'm good," she whispered into the fabric of his shirt.

"You sure?" he asked looking down on

her. “I can take you out of here. We can leave. Hell, I’ll even go kick your father’s ass. All you have to do is say the word. Whatever you want.”

“I need to hear the rest.”

He gave a nod, opened the bathroom door, and guided her back into the study with his hand on her lower back. Edward was standing next to the desk with a bottled water in his hands and a tray full of crackers nearby. “There’s more, but that was the worst of it. I swear.”

She reclaimed her seat and took the water he offered. She took a long swig from the cold liquid hoping it might ease the burn in her heart and her throat.

Edward waited for her to catch her breath, grabbed the file again, and sat down next to her. “I have the newspaper clipping about your mom’s accident, if you’d like to see it.”

“Not yet,” she answered. “Tell me the rest first.”

“Well, you know the family that bought you, and that’s where your story ends and where mine begins.”

“Yours?”

“How I found you,” he answered. “My mother…” He started and then glanced up at Landon. “I’m sure you already did a background check.”

“I did.”

He nodded. “My mother wasn’t

clueless about the affair. She knew about your mother and about you, but she never knew what happened to either of you. My dad told her that he'd broken things off and that she'd vanished with their child."

"And she believed him?"

"No," he answered. "My mother is the whole reason you're sitting here today. Like I said, she knew about the affair, and about the baby, but wanted more answers than what my father was providing. So she did what she does best. She started searching for her own answers. Answers that would make sense. She wasn't always a socialite. She used to be a reporter. She dug up the information on the car accident, and when she read that the woman died but there was no mention of the baby, she started researching what might have happened to you. It destroyed her that your mother died. She didn't view her as competition but as a victim to my father's corruption. That's why she put all her effort into finding out where you were.

"She pulled every string she had to discreetly inquire about you, gathering everything, including a copy of your birth certificate before those records mysteriously ended up in a hospital storage file. She found out that she had terminal cancer the same day she discovered the truth. She'd gone into my father's study to tell him about the cancer, and when he wasn't there, she snooped through his drawers and found the key to his personal safe, which of course she didn't hesitate to open. In that safe, she found your information. He'd been keeping tabs on you since your childhood. She'd found you, and along with that information, she found the thumb drive containing the damning evidence."

"Oh my God. Your mom is the person responsible for the truth coming out."

"Well, technically, I am. She confided in me and gave me the information to try and make things right, but yes, she put it all into motion."

"And your mom?"

"She died." His eyes saddened.

Alice reached for his hand and squeezed. "I'm so sorry."

"Don't be." He squeezed back. "She's smiling down on us. She needed to expose the truth, and she wanted to make sure that you knew as well."

"Unbelievable," she whispered.

"Your father is the reason that hitmen are after her?" Landon asked in atone less than cordial.

"Yes, and my presence guarantees they won't succeed. My father doesn't know that I was responsible for his secrets being exposed He'd never let anyone touch his living heir, although that might change when he realizes I was the instigator in his demise. The only secret left to expose are the players involved." He looked at Alice. "And you. We expose them, and this all goes away."

"Or I kill them, and this all goes away," Landon growled.

"Or that," Edward replied. "Although, if his doctors are to be believed, you won't need to go to all the trouble. Through karma or whatever, he recently found out that he needs a kidney, and I'm not a match."

"What?" she asked. "I hope he doesn't think that I'll be his donor."

"I'm sure you don't have to worry about that," Edward answered. "He pulled your medical history. I found that file, too, and found it before him. I made sure that he knew you weren't a match, even though technically you were. I stripped that opportunity away from him so you, too, wouldn't have an accident since you're an organ donor."

"You did that, for me?"

"Of course." He looked at me. "You're my sister, and personally, I like the idea of our father rotting in prison for the rest of his life."

"What do you get out this if she succeeds?" Landon asked.

Alice lowered her head and closed her eyes, bracing herself for Edward's answer.

"My mother gets her dying wish. Alice's

mother gets justice, and Alice and I get to be family. Nothing more, nothing less."

Alice raised her gaze to his. "Aren't you forgetting your father's companies? You get those too."

"Actually..." Edward stood, rounded the desk, pulled out another envelope, and handed it to her. "I've appointed you my sole beneficiary, so should anything happen to me, everything I own and have, will be yours. I plan to sell off all of his companies and destroy any legacy he's left behind. My plan is to leave no trace of him behind, similar to what he did to your history. I'll be splitting any money that is made with you fifty-fifty. That alone will send my father to an early grave, to know that his bastard child and his son have taken everything away from him in a heartbeat. Nothing would give me greater pleasure than watching his fall."

"Why do you hate him so much?" Alice asked.

Edward's face hardened. "That man destroyed hundreds of lives, including mine. Isn't that reason enough?"

"How did he destroy yours?" Landon asked.

Edward chewed on his bottom lip while he sat quietly debating his answer. If Landon could feel any of the emotion, he didn't say.

"He verbally and physically abused my

mother and me. For that, I'm going to destroy him.

"If you don't want any part in this, I'll completely understand and do it alone. I just found you, and all I'm asking for is a chance to get to know you. That's all."

Chapter 13

Landon lay in the king-sized bed with Alice wrapped in his arms. She'd had a long, emotional day, and he had been counting the minutes until they could be alone.

"Do you believe him?" Landon asked.

"I do," she whispered into the dark room. "Do you?"

"To be honest, I think he's got a lot of daddy issues, and even though I understand where his hate comes from, I'm not comfortable with you being around him by yourself. I don't trust him yet."

Alice drew a circle on his chest. "Do you think he's using me to get back at his dad? Our dad? Dang that still sounds weird."

"I think...he means well, and he's trying to give you the same opportunity to destroy your dad that he has. I think he'll enjoy watching his dad fall."

"What should I do?"

Landon kissed the top of her head and pulled her closer. "Only you can answer that, but whatever you decide, I'll be with you 100 percent. I promised you that."

"You have a lot of promises to keep." She smiled and glanced up at him.

"With you, they're easy to keep."

"He killed my mom."

"I know, baby, and one way or another, he'll pay for that."

Landon could feel the confusion she was going through. It hit him squarely in the chest, as did her despair about finding out what had happened to her mother. She was on an emotional roller coaster, and he was unsure where it would end. He knew only that he would ride it all the way to the end.

"Get some sleep." He kissed her again and let her snuggle into his embrace. Her breathing eased, and his followed.

He'd almost been asleep when she whispered into the dark, "I love you."

"Tell me again when all of this is over and you have a clear head." He kissed the top of her head. "For what it's worth, I love you too."

****

Landon woke with a start, unsure what had pulled him from his sleep. He reached for Alice and shot up straight when he realized she wasn't in bed. "Alice," he called out in the room and glanced at the alarm clock, which read six a.m.

He turned toward the bathroom. The door was open, and that light was off as well. "Crap."

He slid from the bed and hurried to dress. Grabbing his gun, he stashed it in the waistband of his jeans and was yanking the shirt down over his chest as he made his way down the hall. He jogged down the stairs and nodded to the security guy posted at the door. He rounded the banister and headed toward the kitchen. When he heard her voice, he slowed, and his heart started beating again. He entered the kitchen and noticed Edward at the table with a cup of coffee in front of him and Alice pouring herself a cup.

She glanced over her shoulder. "Good morning."

He moved to her side and kissed her neck. “Morning, baby. You should have woken me up.”

“I wanted to let you sleep. You haven’t gotten much since having to babysit me.”

Landon smiled down at her and winked. “You are a handful.” He poured his own cup of coffee and met them both at the table. “So what did I miss? Any more stories?”

“Alice was just about to give me her list of demands.”

“Is that right?” Landon glanced at Alice and leaned back in his chair. “Well, don’t let me stop you, babe.”

Alice cleared her throat. “If I decide to do this, no matter what happens, I don’t want your money or anything from him.”

“Unacceptable,” Edward answered. “You’ll take the money and what you do with it after that is completely up to you. Next demand?”

Alice glanced at Landon and winked. “My next demand is that you and I go to counseling to work on our daddy issues.”

“You want me to see a shrink?”

Landon took a sip of his coffee to hide his smile behind his cup.

“Yes. I think it will be good for both of us, and it might help us form a relationship. This one is non-negotiable. I won’t have any brother of mine turning into a psycho with a god complex.” She grinned at Edward. “Sorry.”

He made a circular motion in the air. “Fine, next.”

“I want birthdays, holidays, family vacations. If I do this with you, I want the whole nine yards. I want to experience having the brother I never had.”

“That doesn’t even count as a demand. That’s a given, but if you need to hear me say it, then I agree.”

“Those will include my sister, Emily.”

“But she’s not your sister,” he countered. “Not by blood. Her family bought you.”

“The sins of the parents are not the sins of the children. I think we can both agree on that. She is a sister to me in every way that matters. She *is* my sister. She was there for me when I scraped my knee or had my heart broken. She’s an innocent victim in all this, just like we are. You either accept us both or neither.”

He took his time to ponder this one. “What if she doesn’t like me? What if she tries to turn you against me?”

“Then we’ll all sit down and discuss the issues as a family. I’m sorry, but this is important to me.”

He gave a slow nod. “Hearing you stick up for her just proves how much I’ve missed out on. I agree to your demand. Anything else?”

“No. I think that about covers it.”

"Good, are you ready for mine?"

"Wait…you have demands?"

"It's only fair."

Landon took another sip of his coffee and watched the comical exchange between the two.

"Sure. It's good that we get everything out on the table."

"Until I know your safety is secure, Landon and you"—he gestured to Landon—"will stay in my home and will have a team of guards with you until every last one of the men responsible are sent to prison."

"Wait, how did I get thrown into this?" Landon argued. "Not that I'd ever leave her to fend for herself."

"That's an easy one. She trusts you. I trust you, and seeing as how you're still leery about me, we kill two birds with one stone. You get extra security to help protect her….even if you're playing kissy face."

"Kissy face." Alice grinned and turned to wink at Landon.

"I can't speak for Landon, since he has a job and a family that need to see him, but I'm willing to stay while everything transpires."

"Perfect." He pulled out his wallet, took a card out, and slid it across the table. "I have set up a trust fund and a bank account with a million in each for your personal use. You haven't been afforded the same opportunities as me, and it's high time that changed."

"I don't want your money," she answered, sliding the card back to him again.

"Non-negotiable." He slid it back. "They are yours. Consider it delayed child support owed to your mother. You will take it, and you will use it as you see fit."

"That's not why I'm here."

"Don't you think I know that?" he answered. "You're my little sister. Let me do this for you."

Alice rolled her eyes. "Fine." She leaned back in her chair and folded her arms over her chest. "What else?"

"I guess, since you tried to return the money, I should probably take the house and the car off the table?"

"You'd be correct."

"Stubborn." He shook his head. "That runs in our family too."

"Good to know. Any other demands I should know about?"

"Nope. I think that about covers it."

"Perfect." She rose from the table. "I need the names of all the major players involved in the cover-up of my mother's murder and the baby trafficking."

"What are you going to do with it when I give it to you?"

Alice smiled at Edward. "Destroy each

and every one of those bastards so I can have my life back. Where will Daddy dearest be at 3 P.M?"

"In court." Edward answered with a grin on his face.

Pride puffed in Landon's chest. Even with the thought of the additional security, they were going to need to keep her safe. She was his, and at that moment, he knew she'd ruined him for any other woman. She had him hook, line, and sinker.

"Operation search and destroy commences at 3 P.M., so you should call in whatever security detail you believe we'll need to get ready for the backlash. I think it's time to give daddy dearest the surprise of his life."

"I like the way you think." Edward stood, pulled out his phone, and started dialing numbers. "I'll tip off the press that there is going to be a breaking story in Dad's courtroom. We'll hit him fast and hard."

Chapter 14

Landon glanced around at all of the news vans crammed into the courthouse parking lot. Edward had come through on getting them assembled on such short notice, with the promise of news that would devastate and turn the country on its head, and Alice wouldn't disappoint. Their security team had canvassed the area for several hours before their scheduled appearance. Edward had gone as far as to call in some serious favors to get the bounty removed from Alice's head, and yet, he still had snipers and ex-military nearby should any trouble occur.

"How do I look?" Alice asked, running her hand down her white dress.

"Like an angel," Landon answered.

Her cheeks tinted the pretty pink that Landon loved. He couldn't be any more proud of Alice than if it were him taking these creeps down. "I've got you," he whispered to her and then kissed her hand. "I've always got you."

"And I've got you back." She winked.

Landon gave a gentle squeeze to her fingers. "Are you ready for this?"

He could feel her apprehension. It rivaled his. He lent her his strength and his confidence when, in reality, it was she that gave him reason to stand at all. To open himself up to his family and friends, to realize he was every bit of the man she needed and deserved. He had saved her life, and she had saved him in return.

Alice lifted her head and nodded toward the bailiff positioned outside the door. She was so strong, so ready. She gave a gentle squeeze and walked through the courtroom doors, and the media cameras turned on her for the first time. Apprehension ate at her spine, yet she lifted her chin, refusing to show any fear. The man that sold her sat regally in his black robe. His hair was greying around the ears, and yet, Alice felt nothing for the man. He might have donated the sperm, but this man would never be anything more.

She cleared her throat and clasped her hands. "Judge Best is the head of the Falcon Group, which is currently running a baby trafficking scheme, and I have the proof." She held the judge's gaze. "Isn't that right, Father?"

The judge's gaze locked on hers, and he rose slowly from his seat. "Young lady, I could have you arrested."

"I don't think so, Dad."

"Judge Best, is this your daughter?" one of the reporters called out.

He denied it. "I've never seen that woman in my entire life."

"Now that....that is not necessarily true. He saw me the day he killed my mother, which, incidentally, is the same day he sold me to the highest bidder." She squeezed her hands together digging her nails into her skin.

Collective gasps filled the air as a team of FBI agents entered the room.

"That's a lie," he said and rapped his gavel as if that would stop her words and make her disappear. "Bailiff, remove her from the courtroom this instant."

"Now, Father, is that any way to talk to your offspring?" Edward asked as he walked in and stopped by Alice's side.

"You! I should have known you'd be behind these lies."

Edward held up a file in his hand. “I can prove everything she’s saying, down to the hit man you hired to kill her mother...and the more recent ones you sent to kill her as well.”

The judge quit talking as he watched the FBI agents approaching his bench. “This is an outrage.”

“You know. I believe I’m the lucky one. I was raised by a man who was a better father than you could have ever been.” She narrowed her eyes, shooting daggers across the room. “I've survived twenty-nine years without you. Without your love, without knowing you were blood. You took my mother away, as if she was trash to be thrown out, and despite it all, despite what you took from me, it's because of you that I have so much more. I don't want your money. I don't want your name. I don’t want anything from you. I have my mother's strength, and her courage, and her conviction. And it’s her qualities in me, the same kind of woman you tried to discard, that will see you rot in hell.”

“Judge Best, drop the gavel and place your hands behind your back. You are under arrest for murder, attempted murder, kidnapping, and human trafficking.”

He did as asked without taking his eyes off Alice. All of the hate that Edward felt toward his father was returned in that single look as he stared at his children, and Landon lifted his chin and smiled.

The courtroom erupted in a matter of seconds as the judge was escorted out the room. Reporters clamored, shouting questions and demanding answers.

Edward stepped forward and held up his hands to quiet the crowds. “I only recently found my sister or I would have come forward sooner. These files have been sent to every one of your news stations and editors. It is despicable what my father has done, and I will not condone his actions or stand by his side. The information has been made public and brought out into the light in the hopes that, should anything happen to my sister or me, the issues will not go away, and those responsible for the travesty will be brought to justice. I have scheduled a news conference, and I will answer all of your questions at that time. Thank you.”

Edward turned and held out his arm in a gesture for Landon and Alice to walk ahead of him.

Alice stepped out of the courthouse, and her eyes locked with the one person she needed. She dropped Landon’s hand and made a dash into her sister’s waiting arms. Both girls cried and held each other, Emily’s words were but a whisper, but Landon could tell by the way she stroked her sister’s hair that things between them would never change, no matter Edward's involvement.

Landon and Edward moved down the steps and toward the sisters. The crowd of onlookers had cameras pointed at the reunion.

"Ladies, I suggest we take this reunion some place more private."

Chapter 15

One month turned into two, and Landon got to spend them with Alice, making sure that she would be okay in her new surroundings. Junior Perriman had been caught and had been charged with killing the parents who'd bought him. All of the families were now accounted for and the men responsible were being handled. The aftermath had been tremendous. The stolen children were now filing suit and having to try and pick up the pieces of their shattered lives. The men responsible were all behind bars and trying to cop a plea for giving each other up. Alice didn't need Landon's protection, not with Emily there to help. It didn't hurt that she was a trained operative and someone Landon trusted.

Landon and Alice stood in the driveway. A limo stood waiting, and it was at this juncture that Landon knew his life would never be the same.

"Are you sure you have to go?" Alice asked, taking both of Landon's hands into hers.

"Yeah," he answered. "I've been given another assignment." He slipped his hands free and cupped her face. "You're good here. You've got Emily and Edward, and everything has settled down."

Alice's eyes searched his. "I don't want you to go."

"Aw, baby." Landon pressed his lips against hers. "You know if I could stay longer, I would. I've got to go handle this new assignment so I can get it out of the way and won't disappoint my brother. Avery and Reed are counting on me to be at their wedding." He kissed her again, this time slowly and with purpose. He didn't want to forget the way she tasted, the way she felt in his arms. "You've got a new life, new family, and you need to stay and find your groove. I get that. I wouldn't dream of pulling you away. It's too soon."

His face softened as he swiped away the tear that slipped free.

"So what now? Is this goodbye?"

He could feel the heartache pouring from her and had to strengthen his resolve. He'd convinced himself that this place, with her siblings, was exactly where she needed to be. "Think of it as a break. You can get things figured out, and at the end of the day, if you still feel the same way about me, then we'll work out the rest."

"Wait." She dropped her hold. "You think that my feelings for you are based on the fact that you saved my life."

Landon wrapped his arms around her waist and pulled her flush to his body. "It wouldn't be the first time that's happened to an operative. But that's not what I'm implying. I'm saying I need you to be sure that I'm what you want. You deserve better than me, baby. You deserve so much more than I could ever give you."

"No..." She shook her head.

"Yes." He kissed her denial away. His heart was breaking into a million pieces. "Be good, and give them hell, Alice."

Landon dropped his hold and moved to the limo. He glanced back at her one last time in an effort to memorize the face of the one woman who would own his heart forever. "I've always got you. You need me, you call."

She stood in the driveway, her arms wrapped around her waist. She didn't give him a reply, only stood watching him. Landon slid into the limo, shut the door, and hid behind the tinted glass. His entire chest felt as if it was about to cave in, even if he knew he was doing the right thing, the honorable thing.

****

A month later, Alice sat in the study like she did every day with her cup of coffee in hand as Edward, Emily and she discussed the status of the charity they'd established for the families affected by their father's horrible deeds. Her gaze was out the window, her mind on the man who had left her and torn her heart into a million pieces. The snow drifted outside, reminding her of a time when it rained flower petals.

"Alice…" Edward's voice broke through the fog.

"What? I'm sorry." She turned her attention back to the conversation. "What were you saying?"

Edward and Emily exchanged a sad, knowing look. "I zoned out for a minute. I'm sorry."

"Where did you go?" Emily asked.

"The snow reminded me of raining flower petals." Her heart clenched remembering Landon's arms wrapped around her while he shared his special place with her. She remembered his words. *You're part of my special place now.*

"Honey." Emily reached over and squeezed Alice's hand. "It doesn't rain flowers. Did you hit your head and not tell us?"

Alice shook away the memories and shoved them out of her mind. "No, I'm fine." And the truth was she was fine. Her heart ached, and the tears had stopped, but she was able to breathe again.

"It's okay that you miss him," Edward started.

"He's a good man to miss," Emily echoed.

"He is…I mean he was," Alice answered. "No, he is."

Edward flipped the portfolio closed on his desk and leaned back in his chair, steepling his fingers together. "I'm calling a family meeting."

"Isn't that what we're doing?" Alice gave him a quizzical look.

"This family can't work without everyone participating."

Alice shot Emily a confused look. "We are participating."

"No. We're not. We're missing a piece of our puzzle."

"He's right, Alice," Emily added.

"Emily?" Alice's mouth parted.

"We'll, it's true." Edward moved around the desk. He perched on the edge, grabbed a white envelope off the surface, and handed it out to her.

"What is this?" she asked, running her finger under the flap. She pulled out Reed and Avery's wedding invitation. There was a sticky note on the front.

Your other invite is full of bullet holes, but you're still expected to be here.

P.S. He's miserable and grumpy, and I hold you responsible. Get your ass back here and fix this. Haven't you both suffered enough!!!!!!

P.S.S. He's a Love man, and they require an extra kick in their ass. Trust me on this.

P.S.S.S. He was trying to do the right thing....stupid....but in his mind it was because he loves you that he let you go. Now don't make me come kick down your door. Get your ass back here.

"I think we have some arrangements to make." Edward lifted up his invite, and so did Emily. They'd all been invited. "Ours had a sticky note too, and let's just say your friend, Avery, uses colorful words. My note included instructions on how to keep my family jewels intact."

"And mine said that she was calling in her favor for saving your life the first time, and if I had to drug you and drag your ass there, that we were not to miss her wedding or the Love family lunch the day before," Emily added.

"And then I got a computer virus. Do you know how to fix this?" he asked and turned his computer around.

Alice rose from her chair and clutched the invite to her chest. Edward's computer screen was filled with pictures of Landon and her. Pictures that were probably taken from all of the hospital and home security cameras, but they showed Landon and her, laughing and smiling with his arms around her and she looking up into his eyes. It showed when they shared breakfast in her office the day she'd delivered the baby. Picture after picture kept popping up of all their time together, and in that instant, tears gathered in Alice's eyes and slipped freely down her face. God, she loved that man.

"I love him," she whispered into the quiet room. "And I let him get away."

Emily rose and put her arms around her sister's shoulders. "Aw, honey, he didn't go far, and after talking with Avery a week ago, it seems he loves you just as much. Trust us on this. Go beat some sense into him, and do not take no for an answer."

"That's our new family motto." Edward grinned and clapped his hands. "I think we all have some wedding presents to buy and reservations to make." He glanced at

Alice and held her gaze. “Are you sure this is what you want? That he’s what you want?”

Alice nodded. “I’ve never been more sure about anything in my life.”

“Then that’s settled. Let’s get our asses in gear.” Emily squeezed her sister’s shoulders.

“You sounded just like Avery.” Alice smiled.

“She was my mentor. I’m not surprised.”

Chapter 16

Landon smiled for the pictures at all the right times during the rehearsal dinner and ignored the onslaught of love that floated around the room. His brothers and sisters were all happy and it wasn't that he begrudged them their relationships. It was that he envied them and what they had, and had found. He'd had it too...once.

"You know you're a stubborn ass," Avery said, sliding up next to him at the bar.

"I've been called worse," he mumbled, lifted the beer to his lips, and took a long, hard pull.

"Have you heard from her?"

Landon shook his head. "No, and I checked the hotels; I don't think they plan to come for the wedding." He glanced at Avery. "Nice try, though. I knew you meant well, and I love you for that."

"Are you going to go get her?"

Landon gave Avery a lopsided grin. "I'm going to do more than that, but not until after the wedding. I'm not sure the family would survive if I bailed on another."

Landon pulled the ring box out of his pocket and slid it across the bar, making Avery squeal in delight, a sound he rarely heard from his soon-to-be sister-in-law. "That was a new sound. I think Sky and Olivia are rubbing off on you."

Avery gave a playful bump to Landon's shoulder and opened the box. Her eyes smiled with approval and delight. "It's okay, if you like big diamonds," Avery teased. "Personally, I love mine more."

"As you should," Reed announced, walking up behind her and wrapping his arms around her waist. "So, do you think she'll take you back? You know it's been a month. She may have gotten over you already and moved on."

"Don't listen to him, Lan. I have a feeling you might be surprised." Avery turned in Reed's arms and kissed him on the lips.

"You two need to get a room and let me drink my beer in peace."

Avery closed the ring box and handed it back to Landon. "You know, I believe giving her that ring will be the smartest thing you've ever done."

Landon chuckled and turned to face his family. "You know, I've trampled through the jungle, dodging bullets at my back. I've fought some of the baddest of the bad, and during those times, I wasn't scared in the least bit." He lifted the ring box. "But this..." He shoved the box into the pocket inside his coat. "The thought of waiting for her answer...scares the shit out of me."

"Well, you know Mom will have a fit if you don't follow tradition and propose like the rest of us...in the backyard."

Landon chuckled, he officially felt at home for the first time in a long time. "Sorry, bro. I have to grab the opportunity wherever I can. I'm not sure she's ever coming back to the island, and to be honest...I'd go with her to the ends of the earth."

****

Edward pulled the SUV up behind all of the other cars in front of the Love family house. Alice twisted her sweaty palms in her lap as butterflies did the tango in her stomach.

"Are you sure they said we were invited?" Alice asked nervously. "Maybe we should just wait till the wedding."

"Don't be ridiculous," he answered.

"I already spoke to Avery," Emily answered. "She's expecting us."

Alice gave a slow nod and let out a shaky breath. "I don't know if I can do this."

"Of course you can. We're both with you." Edward reached for Alice's hand and gaze a slow squeeze.

Within a second, the passenger door flew open, and Avery popped her head in. "Too late to make a run for it." She grinned and reached in to unbuckle Alice's belt. She pulled her out and hugged her. "Thank you for coming."

"I wouldn't miss it." Alice smiled at her friend.

"Landon is in the back. You can go around the house if you want, and I'll take Edward and Emily inside. I'm sure Landon and you have plenty to talk about, and I'll keep the others at bay until you're ready."

"Thanks." Alice smiled and headed into the yard to round the house, leaving her siblings to fend for themselves.

She stepped around the corner and found Landon at one of the tables nursing a beer. His eyes cut to her, and he slowly rose from his seat.

"What are you doing here?"

Alice closed the distance, stopping a foot away before she answered. "Avery threatened sure death if I...we didn't come."

Landon's lips turned down at the corner.

"I can go..." She hitched her thumb over her shoulder. "If you don't want me here, I can leave."

Landon's brows dipped. "I want you here, but if you'd rather go...I hope you say no."

Alice's heart lifted at that moment as she stared into Landon's blue eyes. "I want to stay."

Landon reached for her waist and pulled her flush against his body and wrapped his arms around her. "Thank God." He kissed her hair. "I was coming for you after the wedding."

"You were?"

"Yeah, I had to ask you a question."

"Why didn't you just call?"

Landon looked down into her confused face and kissed her lips in a kiss that made her body relax into his. "I wouldn't have been able to do that."

She smiled. "So you wanted to play kissy face?"

"I want more than that. I want forever."

"What?" she asked breathlessly.

"I love you, Alice Page, and letting you go was the worst decision of my life. I plan to rectify that if you'll have me."

Landon released her, dropped to his knee, and pulled out the ring box, not one for wasting time. "Alice, all this time I've told you that I had you, that all you had to do was call. Well, the truth was you've got me. You've always had me, and I hope that I'll have you."

Hope blossomed and filled her heart. A tear gathered in her eye.

"Marry me. I don't care where we live, where we go, none of that matters if I can have you by my side. You're better than my fantasy of the flower rain. You're my everything."

Landon pulled the ring out and held it up. "Please say yes."

"You're sure about this?" she asked, her voice a whisper.

"Absofuckinglutely." He grinned.

Alice nodded and grinned, holding out her hand. Landon slipped the gold into place and rose, pulling her into his arms in a kiss that was long and well overdue. He spun her around and rained kisses on her face before he put her back on her feet.

"Wait...how did you know I'd be here? How did you plan the ring?"

"I bought it my first day back, and I've carried it with me ever since. I didn't lie when I said I was coming for you. I had every intention of finding you and whisking you away. Nothing would have stopped me from trying to win you back."

"You never lost me, Landon." Alice cupped his cheek. "I've always got your back. I love you, Landon."

"I love you more, baby. Be my family."

She nodded through the tears that slipped free. "Absofuckinglutely."

Landon smiled, and cheers broke out from both the families that had moved and waited patiently on the patio. Hoots and hollers from his brothers and squeals from the girls came from the direction of the house. This day had been about Avery and Reed, and now...they truly had a reason to celebrate. Landon was one hundred percent in love and whole once again.

The End.

Text KATE to 313131 and get a text message on release dates!

Sign up for her newsletters HERE

Other Books by Kate Allenton

Suggested Reading Order

BENNETT SISTERS BOX SET (Books 1-4 in one bundle, 1218 pages)
INTUITION (Book 1)
TOUCH OF FATE (Book 2)
MIND PLAY (Book 3)
THE RECKONING (Book 4)
REDEMPTION (Book 5)
CHANCE ENCOUNTERS (Book 6)
DESTINED HEARTS (Book 7)

PHANTOM PROTECTORS BOX SET (Books 1-4 in one bundle, 964 pages)
RECKLESS ABANDON (Book 1)
BETRAYAL (Book 2)
UNTAMED (Book 3)
GUIDED LOYALTY (Book 4)

CARRINGTON-HILL INVESTIGATIONS
DECEPTION (Book 1)
DEADLY DESIRE (Book 2)

SHIFTER PARADISE BOX SET

NOT MY SHIFTER/ SINFULLY CURSED

KARMA

SOPHIE MASTERSON SERIES/ DIXON SECURITY
LIFTING THE VEIL (Book 1)
BEYOND THE VEIL (Book 2)
VEILED INTENTIONS (Book 3)
VEILED THREATS (Book 4)

THE LOVE FAMILY SERIES
SKYLAR (BOOK1)
DECLAN (BOOK 2)
FLYNN (BOOK 3)
REED (BOOK 4)
LANDON (BOOK 5)
ALEXIS (BOOK 6)
GABE (BOOK 7- COMING SOON)
JACKSON (BOOK 8- COMING SOON)

HELL BOUND
MYSTIC TIDES BOX SET

ABOUT THE AUTHOR

Kate has lived in Florida for most of her entire life. She enjoys a quiet life with her husband, Michael and two kids.

Kate has pulled all-nighters finishing her favorite books and also writing them. She says she'll sleep when she's dead or when her muse stops singing off key.

She loves creating worlds full of suspense, secrets, hunky men, kick ass heroines, steamy sex and oh yeah the love of a lifetime. Not to mention an occasional ghost and other supernatural talents thrown into the mix.

Sign up for her newsletters by going to her website.

She loves to hear from her readers by email at KateAllenton@hotmail.com, on Twitter@KateAllenton, and on Facebook at facebook.com/kateallenton.1

Visit her website at www.kateallenton.com

www.ingramcontent.com/pod-product-compliance
Lightning Source LLC
Chambersburg PA
CBHW071917220626
47052CB00002B/387

* 9 7 8 1 9 4 4 2 3 7 1 5 8 *